# BRIGHT HORIZON

## ROSEMARY HAYES

**Hodder
Children's
Books**

a division of Hodder Headline Limited

Text copyright © 2004 Rosemary Hayes

First published in paperback in Great Britain in 2004
by Hodder Children's Books

A Catalogue record for this book is available from
the British Library

ISBN 0 340 85471 5

J204,125
€9.00

Typeset in Bembo by Avon DataSet Ltd,
Bidford-on-Avon, Warwickshire

Printed and bound in Great Britain by
Bookmarque Ltd, Croydon, Surrey

The paper and board used in this paperback by
Hodder Children's Books are natural recyclable products
made from wood grown in sustainable forests.
The manufacturing processes conform to the environmental
regulations of the country of origin.

Hodder Children's Books
A Division of Hodder Headline Limited
338 Euston Road
London NW1 3BH

*For Tilly, with love*

# 1

**Melbourne, April 1942**

William Harris stretched and yawned as he stared out of the hotel window on to the street outside. It was a fine day but there was a hint of an autumn chill – enough to make his joints creak. He felt tired. He would be seventy-six years old in December. Too old to keep on running this place, especially now that the country was at war and there was the shortage of staff and the whole of the city was full of American soldiers needing feeding and entertaining.

But there was no choice. There was only him and Amy to keep the place going – with whatever help they could get. Nearly everyone was involved in the war effort in some way, either serving in the forces or as nurses, or filling the gaps in industry that had been left by fighting men.

He sighed and let his thoughts drift back to happier times.

Will remembered little of his early life. He only knew that his mother had died when he was born and that when he was just a toddler, his sick grandfather had dumped him at the hotel. That's when he'd first met his father, Amos, who ran the hotel.

Amos had never married Will's mother, he had married Flo, the love of his life, who ran the hotel with him. Will could have resented her, but he never did. Amos and Flo had taken him in and Flo had treated him as her son, even though, later, she had had four daughters of her own. Flo never made him feel that he didn't belong. He had loved her – she was the only mother he remembered. As far as he was concerned, Amos and Flo were both his parents.

Then there was Harriet, who lived with them, the irritable and disfigured half-sister to Amos. Will smiled at the memory of Harriet. She had hated most of the world – except, apparently, Will. Harriet had been sixteen when Will arrived at the hotel and right away she'd taken him under her wing. 'Two misfits,' she'd said, 'who must stick together.'

Flo had said it was only Will's arrival that had made Harriet get out of herself and face the world despite her scarred flesh.

Will had always known her like that – ugly and scarred – though they said she'd been beautiful before the fire. The fire that had swept through the hotel and burnt her so badly.

Henry and Molly, Harriet's parents, were in charge then, but they were long dead now, and Amos and Flo, too.

Harriet, though, had only died a few years back. She'd lived to a ripe old age and her temper had never improved. Will was the only one who had ever seen the softer side of her and he still missed her. He missed her sharp tongue and gimlet eyes. Nothing got past Harriet. She had helped him run the hotel after Amos had died and had ruled the staff with a rod of iron, often upsetting them. It was then left to Will to smooth their ruffled feathers and restore calm. He and Harriet had understood each other, though, and they'd worked happily together over the years, managing to keep the hotel going, despite the terrible Depression in the Thirties.

Will sighed. No doubt Amos had thought that, between all his children and relations, there'd be plenty of heirs to continue to run the hotel, but he'd been wrong; it had not worked out that way. Neither Harriet nor Will ever married, and when Flo's girls grew up, they left and raised families in other parts of the state. They weren't interested in running the place and nor were their children. It was only after strong pressure from Harriet that one of the great-grandchildren had agreed to come and learn the hotel business so that it could be kept in the family.

And so it was that John came into the hotel business.

He was the grandson of Flo's eldest daughter. He'd been born in 1911 and was a clever, good-looking young man who learnt the business quickly and was popular with all the staff.

Everyone was pleased when he married his lovely Amy in 1933 and the young couple moved into the hotel. They were both hard-working and enthusiastic and full of ideas for improvements and changes. And when, in 1934, Amy gave birth to twins, Jane and David, the future of the hotel seemed assured.

Will had felt a huge burden lift from his shoulders. At last, he could begin to hand over the reins.

But then, in 1939, everything changed. War broke out in Europe and suddenly Australia was involved, too. Will had begged John not to join the forces. He'd pleaded with the authorities that John's work at home was essential, but John was determined to 'do his bit'. He'd stayed home for a while but he'd been restless and felt guilty so, eventually, he had gone off to fight, leaving Will and Amy to run the place on their own.

Will's thoughts were interrupted by the thunder of footsteps along the passage and young David burst into the room. At eight, he was a well-built child, with a round face, brown eyes and a thatch of dark brown hair.

'Uncle Will,' he panted. 'Mother says you must come straight away. Quick! There's a fight downstairs.'

David's expression was full of importance. Will patted his head affectionately.

'Who's fighting, son?'

'Some American soldiers! They're fighting over a *woman*!'

Will smiled. Automatically, he reached for his gold watch and chain, to check the time. He had worn it across his chest for years, ever since Amos had given it to him before he died.

Then he stopped himself, irritated. He still reached for it, even though he had given it to John, when John signed up and went off to war.

He'd wanted John to have it, to remind him of the importance of family, of something that had been handed down, through the generations. For John to realize that he had a responsibility to them and, perhaps, to guard him and bring him home safely.

'Come *on*, Uncle Will. They might *kill* each other!'

'Oh, I doubt that very much, David,' said Will. But he allowed himself to be tugged out of the room towards the noise down in the hotel lobby.

Amy met them at the bottom of the stairs. She looked strained.

'I've tried to reason with them, Will, but they won't take it from a woman. Quick, you must stop them before they do any more damage.'

Will observed the scene with a well-practised eye and summed up the situation.

A young woman in nurse's uniform was huddled against the wall, looking frightened, while two American soldiers were lashing out at each other and being urged on by a whole lot more who were crowded behind them.

Will looked about the lobby. Some tables had been knocked to the ground, a few glasses had been smashed, but the damage wasn't too bad.

In his younger days, Will had had a strong, ringing voice. It was weaker now, but it still carried some authority. He stood a little way up the stairs, above the rabble, and yelled with all his might. 'Stop this instant!' he bellowed. 'Or we'll close the doors, take all your names and report you to your commanding officers.'

The two fighting soldiers took no notice, but their comrades had heard.

'And, what's more, I shall ban every one of you from this hotel if you don't clear out NOW!'

Will knew that this was the strongest threat. There were few enough places for the American troops to go in the city and they liked coming here. Amy and Will had soon seen an opening for good cheap food for the troops, though the shortages were cruel and it took all their imagination to find supplies.

There was a shuffling and a murmuring and then, as if by magic, the fighters were separated and hustled out. Gradually, the whole crowd melted away, though one young man hesitated at the door and turned back to Will. 'Sorry, buddy,' he said.

Will nodded. 'No harm done this time,' he replied.

When the soldiers had gone, he and Amy cleared up the mess they'd left behind. The twins helped, too.

As they were sweeping up the broken glass and the contents of spilt ashtrays and putting the furniture to rights, Amy looked up from the floor.

'You can't blame them,' she said.

Will nodded. 'Poor boys have to relax some time.'

Some of those lads will be dead before the war is over, thought Will. Let them live a little now. But he never said this out loud. John was on his mind all the time, and it didn't do to dwell on what might happen to him. As it was, Amy had enough trouble answering the twins' questions.

'Will Daddy come home soon?'

'What's Daddy doing?'

'Why's Daddy fighting the Japs?'

David still questioned Amy constantly, but, as the months went by, Jane had gradually stopped asking after her father all the time. She was a sensitive child and she knew how Amy missed John and knew that the questions upset her.

Will got up slowly. 'Well done,' he said. 'We're shipshape again.'

The twins ran off and Will and Amy sat down to snatch a few moments together. These days they had no time to talk about anything except the running of the hotel. They were down to a skeleton staff to help them – mostly people too old or unfit to serve in the forces – and, what with rationing and shortages and little transport, every day was a struggle.

They discussed plans for the week ahead, making lists and trying to think of ways round all the new regulations imposed by the Government.

'I keep phoning the rail station to see if our deliveries have come down from the country, but I can't get through and we're running really short,' said Amy, pinning up a loose strand of hair as she spoke.

'They'll be busy sorting out all the troops, I expect,' said Will. 'Tell you what, I'll take a stroll down to the station myself.'

Amy smiled at him gratefully. 'Thanks, Will,' she said. 'I'll have more time tomorrow. The children are back at school then.'

Will nodded, then he got up and made his way over to the cloakroom to fetch his hat and stick. He walked slowly out of the main door and into the sunshine.

The walk to the station was short, but Will took his time, looking around him as he went. How things had changed in the past months. Ever since Darwin was bombed in February, the war had moved closer to home. The Australian mainland was under threat of invasion now and Melbourne had been transformed.

Only dimmed lighting was allowed; there were constant air-raid drills, and people in uniform and military cars and lorries all over the place.

As he walked, Will hardly bothered to glance at the shop-fronts. Most of them had been boarded up or had wire netting over them and there was precious little to buy. There were people everywhere, some patiently queueing, some rushing to their destinations and many trying to board the crowded trams. Everyone was affected by the war.

Will had to walk round a ladder where a man was pasting up a wartime poster – 'Careless Talk Costs Lives' it read. It was going up beside two others, one urging people to 'make do and mend' and the other to buy war bonds. Sandbags were another hazard, piled up against buildings and sticking out on to the pavement.

He reached the railway station at last, but he had to force his way through the crowds to get to the office where he could check whether the train bringing their supplies had got through. He felt very old as he watched all the young men and women seething about him, many clinging to each other in tearful farewells. Since the bombing of Darwin many more people had rushed to join the services.

Will finally managed to get to the clerk's office. He leant against the door for a moment to catch his breath. Just as he was turning to go inside, he caught sight of an officer he recognized, but he didn't try to attract his attention. The poor man would have plenty else on his mind. But it took Will back. The officer was one of the Delaware boys, from Flo's side of the family, and he'd last seen him at Harriet's funeral. It had been good of him to come, for Harriet was no relation. It must have been some remembered loyalty to Flo which had brought him there.

When Flo Delaware had married Amos, secretly, her family, who were one of the richest in Melbourne, had cut her off without a penny and her father had disowned her. But after he died, Flo was reunited with her family and gradually a succession of relations had visited the hotel. Will remembered how happy Flo had been when, at last, they had accepted Amos and their girls.

Will turned the handle of the door and walked inside the office. The one telephone was ringing constantly, but no one answered it. The clerk looked up and smiled. He was quite an old man, but that was pretty normal now that so many people had come out of retirement to help keep things running.

'Good morning, sir.'

'Morning,' replied Will. 'Any news of the freight train from Bendigo?'

The clerk shook his head. 'Sorry, sir, it's chaos here. Nothing's running to time. Trains all taken up with troops again.'

Will shrugged. 'Can't be helped. I'll call in again later.'

'I'll telephone the hotel if you like, sir, when it arrives.'

Will brightened. 'Sure you're not too busy?'

The clerk shook his head. 'Can't have you running up and down from the hotel to the station all day, at your age,' he said.

Will smiled to himself. He doubted the clerk was much younger than him. Aloud he said, 'Thank you. That would be very kind.'

As Will fought his way back out into the street, his mood lightened. Despite all the grimness of war, people seemed to care about each other more and take trouble to be helpful.

He straightened his shoulders and walked a bit faster on the way back to the hotel. Across the road from it, he stopped for a moment, as he always did, surveying it with an owner's pride.

It was a fine building. A good little business which had been handed down from Henry and Molly to Amos and Flo and then to him and Harriet. He mustn't let all that hard work count for nothing. But, to be honest, its survival was in John's hands now, not Will's. So John *must* survive.

The next day, the twins went back to school and more supplies came in from the country at last. These days, they used the horse and cart to fetch stuff from the rail station. Petrol was rationed so they only used the van when it was really necessary.

Amy, Will and the elderly hotel porters were kept busy unloading supplies and checking lists. It was hard work trying to do all this as well as run the hotel, which was full to bursting with military personnel and their relations as well as the normal visitors just looking for a place to sit down for a while and snatch a drink or a meal.

At lunch-time, Amy had to supervise in the kitchen. They had a temporary cook who was bad-tempered and couldn't take even the mildest criticism.

'Will,' said Amy, later, 'We're going to *have* to find another cook.'

Will frowned. 'I know. But where?'

Amy raised her eyes to the ceiling. 'I've no idea, but this one can't cook and she's rude to the rest of the staff. They won't put up with it. It's not as if there's a shortage of jobs. They'll leave and go to the ammunition factory in Footscray. They're crying out for staff there.'

The whole day was full of crises like that and it was a relief when the children came in from school, full of their first day back after the holidays.

'We've got a new teacher, Mum, and she's really *old*!' said Jane.'And tomorrow someone's coming in to teach us first aid and then next week someone's coming to teach us about cammer-something nets.'

'Camouflage nets,' said Amy, smiling.

David interrupted. 'And d'you know *what*, Mum?'

'What, David?'

'They've dug *trenches* in our *playground* and we're going to go and hide in them when the bombs drop!'

'Oh, and Mum . . .' This was Jane again. 'One day soon, we're all going to go to Abbotsford and collect logs to burn in the winter.'

Will watched their eager faces. Such innocent talk. How could the twins possibly understand the horror that was war? To them it spelt excitement and change and learning about new things.

And, again, his thoughts turned to John. What of *his* war? What was he doing? And where *was* he?

### Burma, September 1942

They were having a brief rest before starting work again. John had taken sips from his water bottle but he couldn't even keep this down and he turned and retched into the undergrowth beside the railway line.

He was very frightened.

He wasn't frightened of the heavy manual labour – slave labour really – but he was frightened because he knew he was ill. He'd seen it in other men in the camps and he'd seen how the Japs still forced them to work – until they dropped.

It had been a mess, his war. His unit had arrived in Singapore in January and, only a few weeks later, they found themselves prisoners, confined in the infamous Changi prison camp. He'd always been hungry in Changi – like everyone else – but he'd kept reasonably well.

He sighed. It was because he was one of the fittest that, after a few months, he and some others had been rounded up by their Japanese captors and taken north into Burma to help build the Burma–Thai railway.

It was dreadful work, even for the strongest men, and the prisoners were fed so little they hadn't the energy needed for it. Everyone looked out for each other but, what with moving on up the line all the time, with people dying or being left behind through sickness, you seldom got to know anyone well.

But there was one exception. Ernest Liddle had been with him all the time. Ernest was an Englishman and, like John, he had been chosen from Changi to go up to Burma. Somehow, they'd been moved together, from camp to camp. Ernest sat beside him now.

'Try and keep some water down,' he whispered.

John shook his head. 'I can't.'

'Just a few sips. You must have a little.' Ernest held the water-bottle to John's lips but, try as he might, John couldn't swallow.

Ernest moistened John's lips. Then the whistle blew.

Ernest got to his feet and helped John up. He could hardly stand. Automatically, they both looked towards the nearest Japanese guard, standing a few yards away, a long horsewhip in his hand, with which he was tapping his boots.

'Only two more hours to go,' whispered Ernest. 'I'll do the heavy work.'

John swayed on his feet and bit his lip. Then, with a superhuman effort, he forced himself to lean over the track and secure bolts while Ernest dragged the heavy wooden sleepers into place.

The jungle beyond swam before John's eyes, now coming closer, now receding into the background. He bit his lip again and glanced at the guard. He must not faint and fall over. This was one of the vicious guards and he'd seen what he did to the prisoners who fell down.

He thought back to Melbourne, to his lovely Amy and the twins. To the hotel and his future there, which had seemed so bright. He must get well. Somehow he must get well again so he could get back to them.

Ernest half-carried him back to camp at the end of the day and laid him gently in the shade. He and some others tried to get a little of the meagre food down him, but John was exhausted. He kept drifting off into a fevered sleep and resented the others urging him to try to eat. He wanted peace; just a few hours' respite from this steamy heat and the insects that crawled over them all.

A few hours later he was shaken awake. The tropical night was black and menacing, with occasional squeals from the jungle beyond. John groaned and turned over, but Ernest wouldn't let him alone. He shook him again.

'Listen carefully, John. Have you got anything you can sell?'

John's mind swam back to unpleasant, fevered consciousness. 'What?'

Ernest whispered into his ear. 'I'm going to get out of the camp and go down to the village,' he said. 'I must get you some medicine. They'll know what you need. But I've got to have something to give them in exchange.'

'You can't leave camp!' said John, his voice weak and agitated. 'If you get caught, they'll shoot you.'

'I can look after myself,' said Ernest. 'It's been done often enough. I've seen other guys slip out at night and come back without being seen.'

'And others have been killed,' said John. He heaved himself up on to his elbow. 'Please, please don't do this.'

'I've made up my mind,' said Ernest. He emptied the contents of John's kit-bag on the ground and started to feel the small heap of personal possessions.

'Come on, John, help me. It's pitch black and I can't

see a thing. Is there anything here of value? What about a watch or a cigarette case? Anything they might want?'

John's brain was sluggish. He felt his wrist, but there was no watch on it. Had he sold it in Changi for some extra ration of something? He couldn't remember.

Ernest's hand closed on a smooth round object with a chain attached. 'My God, John! This is a watch and chain. This must be worth something!'

John smiled. His mind was elsewhere, floating away into the past. 'Old Will,' he muttered. 'Old Will gave it to me. God knows why. Stupid bloody thing to haul round with me.'

Ernest put the watch and chain in the pocket of his shorts.

'I'm going to take this to the village, John. Is that all right? Do you mind if I sell it?'

But John was losing consciousness.

For a few moments, Ernest couldn't decide. It was probably quite valuable, perhaps he shouldn't sell it. But then he made up his mind. Surely John's life was more valuable, and if he didn't have some help soon, he would die.

Morning broke and, for a few wonderful moments, John thought he was back in Melbourne. He reached out for Amy, but when he opened his eyes they were met by Ernest's anxious stare.

'Here, mate, have some of this.'

Ernest forced some powder between his teeth, then he put the water-bottle up to his lips. 'You must swallow, old man. This will get you better.'

John tried his best and swallowed a little, but his throat was so dry that most of it came up again. He forced himself to sit up.

'They didn't shoot you?' he rasped foolishly.

Ernest smiled. 'No, I was lucky this time.'

'Did you sell the watch?' whispered John.

Ernest frowned. 'No. I met some other guy who knew you were ill. He gave me a bit of money so I didn't have to sell it.' He paused.

'Anyway, I don't think I could have sold it,' he said suddenly. Then, when John didn't answer, he went on, 'When I reached the village, I looked at it properly. It's a valuable piece, John . . . and have you read the inscription on the back?'

John had his eyes shut, but he shook his head.

'It was given to some bloke called Frobisher, from his father.'

John didn't respond.

'My mother's name was Frobisher, before she married,' said Ernest quietly. 'Somehow, when I saw that, I couldn't sell it.'

Ernest thought that John hadn't heard any of this, but suddenly John opened his eyes. He could hardly speak through his parched lips, but he managed to whisper.

'Then, if anything happens to me, you must have it.'

Ernest shook his head. 'No, mate. That wouldn't be right.'

'Please. Say you'll keep it.'

Ernest didn't answer. He was too choked up to speak.

# 2

## Bedford, April, present day

*F* *or the first couple of days after Mum's car crash, I*
*couldn't do anything – certainly not write a diary, but*
*Gran's been nagging me to keep at it. She says it will take*
*my mind off things, so I've started again. Scribbling away*
*while I sit here in the hospital, willing Mum to get better –*
*to come back to us.*

*It's so cruel. Just as things had turned the corner for us all*
*– and then this happens.*

*Gran says I spend too much time at the hospital but*
*I can't keep away. Mum's been unconscious for nearly a*
*week now and I want to be here when she wakes up.*
*I'm sure she will wake up; I can't bear to think that she*
*won't and, anyway, Gran says we've got to stay positive,*
*that Mum will sense it if we give up on her. So, I'm*
*not going to go down that road. Mum's going to wake up*
*– soon.*

*I'm certain that Keith must have had something to do*
*with the accident. Mum's such a careful driver and anyway,*

there was no other car involved. I bet, somehow, he caused all this. It would be just like him.

I tried to talk to Gran and Grandad about it, but it's difficult to explain. They know about Keith, of course, but they don't know the half of it. They know he wanted to marry Mum and that he's sick in the head and holds some sort of grudge against us all. But they don't know how he tricked Matt into that huge debt; I don't want to drag all that up and worry them. All they know is that Matt's got a recording contract with a record company in London. They don't know that Matt owed Keith all that money and that the record company have repaid every penny.

So Keith has no hold on us any more. But he'll still try and get back at us and that's why I'm sure that somehow he's caused this dreadful accident.

I know Keith's behind it. I just know it. He's dangerous and he's nuts. And if he can't have Mum then he's determined that no one else will either. J204.125

Matt's gone back to London. We all told him to. He's the family star and he's got the chance of a lifetime now, with the new recording contract. We all want him to succeed, just as much as Keith wants him to fail.

I've spent a long time just staring at the hospital walls, trying to think clearly, but it's so hard with Mum lying there, breathing regularly but with her eyes shut and making no response when I squeeze her hand or talk to her.

Where's she gone? Will she ever be the same again, even if she does come round?

*How* dare *Keith do this to her.*

*But how can I prove he's behind this, when there's no evidence? All I have is the threatening letter he sent to Mum that she threw away and Katie and I saved from the rubbish. Not much to go on. But if I don't do something about Keith, he's going to threaten our family for ever.*

*The holidays will be over soon and I've got my exams coming up in the summer. How can I concentrate on exams with Mum like this and Keith lurking out there somewhere, trying his best to ruin us?*

*I'm on my own. I can't expect Matt to help when things are so exciting for him right now. I just hope he remembers to be careful. He's still in danger. We all are.*

## Melbourne, December 1942

It was a blistering hot day. Amy had been in the kitchen all morning supervising the cooking. She was behind the desk now, trying to make sense of the bookings, which had been muddled by a temporary clerk. She peered round the crowded lobby but she was so tired that all the soldiers lounging about were an indistinct blur. They all looked the same. They changed every day, of course, but she could no longer identify them. To her they were just a sea of young men with eager faces, all dressed in uniform, either back on leave or about to go off and fight. This unreal situation had become normal. It was hard to remember what life had been like before the war.

She stretched her aching back. Somehow she must try to make Christmas special – for the sake of the children at least. It would be their second Christmas without their father.

Her thoughts were interrupted by the sound of her name being called. It was the old porter at the front of the hotel. Next to him stood a young boy. Amy smiled over in acknowledgement, but then she saw what the boy was holding. All thoughts of Christmas, of muddled bookings, of problems with the staff, were forgotten. Her mind went blank.

She never knew how she forced herself to walk across the lobby towards them. The porter was looking at her, his face desperately anxious. And she was dimly aware of the other people – all the unknown crowd of soldiers – falling silent as she reached the boy and spoke to him.

'Is that for me?' she said quietly.

The boy nodded silently, handed her an envelope and then slipped out of the door, glad to be away.

Amy held the telegram between her finger and thumb, but she didn't open it. She put it in her pocket and walked slowly up the stairs to the privacy of her bedroom.

After a few moments, the buzz of conversation started up again. The old porter left his post and hurried to the office at the back. He knocked at the door and hardly waited for Will's gruff 'Come in'.

'Sir, you'd better come,' said the porter.

'What? Why?' Then, seeing the look on the man's face, 'Is something the matter?'

'Amy's had a telegram,' said the porter.

Will jumped to his feet at once. 'Amy? Oh God! Oh no. Where is she?'

'She went upstairs, sir.'

Will rushed up the stairs as fast as he could, puffing and panting as he forced his old body to respond to the urgency he felt.

At Amy's door, he hesitated. There was no sound coming from inside. Gently he knocked.

Still there was no sound, so he turned the doorknob and went in.

She was sitting on the bed, the telegram on her lap. She looked up as he entered and as soon as he saw her face, he knew what it said.

Heavily, Will sat down beside her. Gently he took her hand and squeezed it.

And then she started to weep, great heaving sobs that tore at Will's heart.

Will wanted to weep himself, but he knew that one of them must be strong. Carefully, he picked up the telegram and read it, the words blurring in front of his eyes.

It was the news they had dreaded for so long.

John was dead.

He drew Amy towards him and stroked her hair.

As he looked over the top of her head at the opposite wall, he tried to see into a future without John. Would they be able to go on without him? Would they be able to keep this place going so it could be handed on to Jane and David?

He shook his head sadly. His health wasn't good and he was exhausted. So was Amy.

How could they go on like this, now that there was no John to come back and help them? For all these months they'd been saying to each other, 'When John comes back, we'll do this – or that – or the other.' Not a day went by when his name wasn't mentioned.

Now he would never come back. And what would happen to the hotel? The hotel founded by Henry and Molly and Amos and Flo and built up into a thriving concern that had survived the great Depression, when so many other businesses had failed. Would it all have to go?

The weeks that followed the news of John's death were very hard. Amy was unnaturally quiet. Conscientiously, she carried on doing all her jobs and supervising the staff, the supplies and the kitchen, but there was no lightness to her step, no enthusiasm. Dutifully she enquired about the children's school activities and friends, but they were quick to sense her lack of any real interest.

Will watched her carefully, worried that she might be overdoing it. But he could be of little help: his age had caught up with him. If it hadn't been for Jane and David, he'd have given up altogether.

The twins were what kept them all going. There were tears and misery about their father, but their natural energy and good humour won through and, after all, plenty of their school friends were in the same situation. Every day someone they knew received bad news – about a father, a brother, an uncle.

Jane didn't ask about John's death; she kept her thoughts to herself. But sometimes David would catch Will unawares with an unnerving question.

'He didn't die in a battle, did he?' Somehow, to David, it would have been easier to understand if his father had died fighting.

'No, son, he got ill because he had to work very hard and he didn't have enough food to keep going, and no medicines, either.'

The information about John's death had been brief and factual. Rumours had got back to Australia about the infamous Burma railway, but it was difficult to imagine the horrors of it from the relative safety of Melbourne.

Sometimes Amy would say to Will, 'I wish we knew more. I wish . . .'

'It's no good, Amy. I doubt we'll get more information until this dreadful war is over.'

She often questioned soldiers that came to the hotel. But the answer was always the same. The gangs working on the Burma railway were all prisoners of war. They wouldn't be released until the end of the fighting. If they survived that long.

Once, after a long, hard night's work, while Amy and Will were finalizing the day's accounts in the office, she suddenly said, 'Will. That gold watch you gave John. Do you think we'll ever get it back?'

Will had often had the same thought, but he'd said nothing about it. 'I doubt it, my dear.'

Amy closed the book in front of her and looked across the table at him. 'Tell me again, Will. What was the story about the watch? I was never clear how you came to have it.'

Will smiled. 'Do you really want to know?' he asked. Then, when she nodded, he suddenly realized that, if he didn't tell her about it, just as he had told John, no one would know the story behind the watch – and that it was the reason why Henry, the founder of this hotel, had come to Australia in the first place.

So, slowly and carefully, he retraced the history of the gold watch and chain. He told Amy how Henry, then called Jim, had been falsely accused of stealing it and, at the age of twelve, had been transported from London to a boys' penitentiary in Tasmania. How he had served his time and returned to London, bent on revenge. How he had tracked down the real thief and acquired the watch himself. And then how he had fallen into a life of crime and escaped the law by joining the crew of a ship going back to Australia. But this time, with a changed identity, he'd made something of himself and built up the hotel business, first in the Gippsland goldfields and then here in Melbourne.

'Did you ever know Henry?' asked Amy.

'Oh yes, I remember him,' said Will. 'But I was only a young lad when he died. He didn't tell me all that. It was his son, Amos – my father.'

'Amos gave the watch to you, didn't he?'

'Yes, he gave it to me not long before he died and he told me its story then.'

'Wasn't there some inscription on the back?'

Will nodded. 'It belonged to a man called Frobisher. It was stolen from him in the market in London where Henry worked as a lad.'

'But not by Henry?'

Will shook his head. 'No. As I say, Henry was falsely accused.'

Amy sighed. 'Just think,' she said. 'None of your family would have come to Australia if it hadn't been for that watch.'

Will fell silent. Would they ever see it again? He supposed it didn't matter, when young men were dying in their thousands. What was a lost watch? It was of no importance.

Still, it was a part of their family history. It would be sad if it was lost for ever.

### Bedford, April, present day

*Matt rang last night. Actually, he rings most nights to ask after Mum. When I think of those months after he ran away from home, when Mum and I had no idea where he was, it seems amazing that he's got where he has. We're so proud of him. He's come through and he's done it on his own. And now he's doing what he's good at and he's really happy.*

*Well, as happy as he can be, with Mum lying unconscious in hospital and Keith still lurking out there like a ticking time-bomb.*

*I came home from the hospital at lunch-time. My best friend, Katie, was at my house. She'd rung earlier to say that she was going to camp there if necessary until I came back and then she was going to take me to the movies or something.*

*She's been a star, has Katie. She's the only one who knows the whole sorry saga, beginning with Dad dying, then Mum meeting Keith — God, what a disaster that was, none of us ever dreamt how he would affect us all — then Keith taunting Matt, then Matt being accused of stealing equipment from school and running away from home. And none of us knowing for months where he was. Then finding Matt again, and*

Katie and me setting up the gig for his band so that the London record people could hear them.

Katie knew all about Keith's loan shark company, too, and how they'd tricked Matt and the rest of the band into borrowing money they could never repay.

It was good having Katie at my house, with Gran and Grandad. She was great with them and told them all the things they wanted to hear – like how she was sure that Matt was going to be famous, and that I would sail through my exams in the summer (some hope, unless I do some revision, still it pleased the oldies, I suppose) and our plans to take a gap year after A levels.

I sat open-mouthed. At the moment I can't think beyond tomorrow. These gap-year plans are news to me.

Later, when we'd finished lunch and I was alone with Katie, I said, 'I thought you and lover boy had plans to travel after A levels. I don't want to be a gooseberry, thanks very much!'

Katie grinned. 'I've dumped him,' she said. 'I'm off boys! Anyway, it's ages away. We'll still be friends in two years' time, won't we? Who knows about boyfriends! It's no good planning on going overseas with a bloke.'

We went to see a rubbish film but it was so bad it was funny. It's the first time I've really laughed properly since the accident. Just for an hour or so, I forgot all about our troubles.

But when we came out of the film, it all came back in a rush.

'What am I going to do about Keith, Katie?'

*Ever practical, she steered me into a café and ordered a couple of Cokes. When we were sitting down, she said, 'We'll make a plan.'*

*'What sort of plan? What do you mean?'*

*'Well, have you told the police about that threatening note Keith sent your mum?'*

*'No but . . .'*

*'You've still got it, haven't you?'*

*'Yes, but . . .'*

*'Have you shown it to your gran and grandad?'*

*'No . . . I didn't want to worry them.'*

*'Then, the first thing you do is to show it to them and get them on-side. Then you tell the police.'*

*I was shocked. This was scary stuff.*

*'But if we get the police to check up on Keith, he'll get back at us, Katie. You know what he's like!'*

*'Sweetie, he's going to get back at you whatever. He's mental. You've said so yourself.'*

*'But . . .'*

*'Stop saying "but", for heaven's sake. We can't do it ourselves, can we? We don't know where he lives or anything.'*

*'We know the name of his company,' I said slowly. 'Perhaps we could trace him through that.'*

*'And what would you do, if you did find out where he lived?'*

*I shrugged.*

*'Exactly! Believe me, it's better to come clean to your gran*

*and grandad. Tell them everything and then go to the police.'*

*I frowned. If Keith thinks we're involving the police, there's no knowing what he'll do. Katie hasn't lived with him. I have and I know what he's capable of.*

*'Let me think about it,' I said.*

*'Don't think too long,' said Katie.*

*I was still churning all this over in my mind when I went back to the hospital in the evening. Gran and Grandad had been in all afternoon, so I was on my own.*

*I walked slowly into the room, sat down by the bed and took Mum's hand.*

*'What shall I do, Mum?' I whispered to her. 'Shall I go to the police?'*

*There was no response, of course, and I stroked her hair. Someone must be looking after it, I thought, because it was still clean and glossy, just as it had always been.*

*Then, quite suddenly, there was a slight noise. A little grunt. She'd made noises before, but somehow this was different. I leant forward, frowning with concentration.*

*She moved her head a little and grunted again. Then, very slowly, she opened her eyes.*

*'Mum!'*

*She couldn't focus on me, I'm sure of that, but when I said her name, her lips twitched.*

*She was trying to smile!*

*I told the nurse about it and she was brilliant, really encouraging.*

*'The more you talk to her, the better,' she said. 'Say*

anything that comes into your head. Just so she hears a familiar voice.'

So I chatted on for ages, about nothing really.

She didn't open her eyes again, but the memory of that smile was so vivid and I left the hospital on cloud nine, longing to rush home to tell Gran and Grandad.

And then, as I walked to the bus stop, I saw him. Keith.

He was standing in the shadows, smoking a cigarette. I don't know if he saw me or not. I legged it and managed to hop on a bus that was just leaving.

I was still shaking when I got to the stop at the end of our street and I ran all the way up to the house, fumbling the key in the door. When at last I got it open, I slammed it shut behind me and leant against it, my heart pounding.

# 3

## Melbourne, April 1947

Jane sat in her bedroom looking at all the clothes piled neatly on her bed. Then at the big trunk on the floor with its lid open. It looked very large and very empty. Somehow she couldn't bear to start packing. But it was her own fault. She'd said she wanted to do it herself, so her mother had agreed. She sighed and kicked the lid shut. Then she went out of the room and along the passage to David's room. For a moment she stood at the doorway looking in.

David was mooching about, taking no interest in the packing, while Mum was neatly placing shoes, trousers, thick woollens and all sorts of unfamiliar items into his trunk.

David saw Jane and raised his eyes to heaven. 'Have you seen these *clothes*?' he said, pointing at a pile of heavy underwear which hadn't yet made its way into the trunk.

'You'll thank me for packing them, David, you mark

my words,' said Amy. 'The climate in England is very different from the climate here in Australia.'

'But I thought you said it would be summer when we get there?'

'Ah yes, but still, English summers aren't the hot summers you are used to, dear.'

Amy had never been to England herself, but she had heard stories about the cold, wet climate and she was taking no chances.

Jane felt miserable. She didn't want to go on this trip. She didn't want to leave her friends in Melbourne and go to some school in England. She was dreading it.

David just thought it was all a big adventure, but Jane was scared. Scared of the long boat trip, scared of going to a strange country, scared of changing schools. Scared of everything.

Mum had been preparing for this for months. Ever since old Will died and she'd given up running the hotel, she'd planned on going to England. Before his death, Will had rambled on and on about tracing his English ancestors and he'd made Mum promise that, one day, she'd go there and try to find them. But Jane thought Amy had just been humouring the old man; she never thought that her mother would honour the promise.

Gradually it had developed into a concrete plan and Jane finally realized that Amy was serious and that it really was going to happen. She had pleaded, then, to be left in Melbourne.

'Please, Mum, I'm thirteen now. I want to be with my friends. You and David go, but let me stay here, please.'

But Amy was adamant. 'Leave you behind and let you miss out on the trip of a lifetime? Whatever next!'

So, Jane had no choice but to go along with Amy's plans. But she wasn't happy. She'd talked to her teacher about England and she knew how bad things were there. After all, it was only two years since the war had ended and apparently there were bombed-out buildings everywhere and rationing and shortages. It sounded a grim place.

And it wasn't as if Mum *knew* anyone there – except this man Ernest Liddle. And she'd never actually *met* him. They'd just written letters to each other.

Jane vividly remembered the day Mum had first heard from Ernest Liddle. Ernest had been a prisoner with Dad in Burma and he'd been with him when he died. Mum and old Will had pored over the letter and read it out to the twins. Jane had heard it so often that, even now, she could remember it, almost word for word:

'. . . *wanted to let you know that John talked of you all the time . . . he died peacefully and we saw to it that he had a Christian burial. He insisted that I look after his gold watch and chain and I have it with me still. But I should like to return it to the family. . .'*

Both Amy and Will had been pleased that the watch and chain were safe – there was some bit of family history attached to it, apparently.

Of course, Amy had written back then. She wanted to know every detail about John's time in Singapore and in Burma, but Ernest Liddle hadn't given her many details, no matter how often she asked for them. So she started to build a fantasy about going to meet this man to find out more, face to face. That's how it all began, two years ago, when she'd first heard from him. And as Will got sick and kept on about tracing his ancestors in England – who were John's ancestors, too, of course – her plans had started to take shape. She would honour her promise to Will and she would meet up with Ernest Liddle.

So, after Will died and she decided to stop working in the hotel, she had started talking to the children about her plans.

Mum's voice broke into Jane's thoughts.

'Have you finished your packing, Jane? You need to get a move on, dear. We're sailing tomorrow, you know. Not next week!'

Jane nodded, but she stayed where she was. She knew she couldn't stop this trip now. Everything had been arranged, but she wished with all her heart that she wasn't going.

Still, one thing was good. Organizing the trip had taken Mum out of herself. Ever since she'd made up her mind to go, she'd been excited and enthusiastic, and some of this had rubbed off – at least on David.

Jane turned to go back to her packing. Well, maybe it *would* be a big adventure. Maybe she would enjoy it, after all.

But it was with a heavy heart that she hauled the heaps of clothes off her bed and stuffed them into the huge trunk.

There'd been so many changes in the past year or so. Old Will dying, Mum selling up the hotel, meeting all the relations who had to have their share. Endless talk with lawyers. Jane wondered, really, if Mum should have sold it, but no one else wanted to take it on.

They should have made a lot of money from the sale, but once the relations had had their cut, and the lawyers theirs, there wasn't that much left. And it was just after the war – nobody wanted to buy anything – so the hotel had gone at a knock-down price.

Then they'd moved to this house in South Yarra. Jane had nothing against the house, it was lovely, but she missed the hotel. The hustle and bustle, all the staff she had known so well. They'd been like family to her. Now they'd all gone out of their lives.

Now Mum was taking them away from everything else that was familiar.

And she wouldn't say how long they'd be away.

'We'll see, dear. But we need to stay a few months, at least, to make it worth the trip.'

A few months! So much could happen in a few months.

Would they ever come back to Melbourne?

That evening, when all the final arrangements had been made, when the couple who were to mind the house while they were away had come and been settled in, Amy took the children for a last drive round Melbourne.

'We know where everything is,' said David, impatiently. He didn't want to go on this drive down memory lane.

And nor did Jane. She wanted a last chance to see her friends.

But Amy insisted. She drove back into the city in the family car they'd had when John was alive. New cars were still hard to come by and, anyway, she was fond of this old one. As they passed landmarks, she pointed them out to the children, as if they didn't know them, and when they reached the hotel, she stopped the car across the street and looked long and hard at it, but she said nothing.

Jane stared at it, too. She'd never forget it. Nearly all

her life so far had been spent inside its walls. It held so many happy – and sad – memories for her.

Why was Mum doing this? Did she think they'd never see it again?

At last, when it was getting dark, they drove slowly home.

'Tomorrow our adventure begins,' said Amy.

'Hurrah!' shouted David.

But Jane said nothing.

The next day passed in a blur of piles of luggage, final farewells, crowds on the dockside, new smells, new sights.

Even Jane felt a stirring of excitement when, at last, they were on board the huge liner which was to take them to England. She and David explored every inch of their cabins and the lounge and recreation areas. Jane was amazed. There was so much to do and there were so many people all going to England. She noticed several children milling about with their parents, and she suddenly felt less isolated and began to relax.

When, at last, the ship slid out into the water and across Port Phillip Bay, she stood at the rail with Amy and David and waved and waved until the people on the dockside were tiny dots.

The rest of the day was spent unpacking and exploring and then, in the evening, they changed for dinner.

Jane was no stranger to dining-rooms. She'd been brought up in an hotel, after all, and she and David had sometimes been allowed to have a meal in the dining-room, as a treat. But the one on the ship was very grand and she couldn't help noticing that there weren't many children there. They'd obviously had to eat earlier.

And she couldn't help noticing, either, that people gave them admiring glances when they came in. Amy sparkled with excitement – no longer the care-worn mother, constantly tired and worrying about the hotel. She looked young and glamorous and seeing her mother like this made Jane realize how exhausted Amy had been and why she had needed to get right away from her old life. At least for a while. Jane felt really proud of her.

That first night, they sat at a big long table for dinner, with a lot of the other passengers. Everyone seemed to want to talk to Amy, but Amy always included her children in the conversation.

When, at last, they made their way down to their cabins for the night, Jane squeezed her mother's hand. 'You looked lovely, Mum.'

Amy smiled. 'Thank you, darling,' she said simply. Then she added, 'I know you didn't want to come, but I had to get away for a while. Do you understand?'

Jane nodded. She did understand now.

'And I couldn't have gone without you both. I would have been so miserable.'

David had run on ahead but he stopped and looked back. 'This is terrific,' he shouted. 'I like being at sea.'

Amy smiled. 'I knew you would,' she said. Then she tucked her arm through Jane's. 'I knew you both would.'

David went straight to his cabin, but Jane and Amy were sharing and they sat up for a long time that evening, talking to each other in a way they'd never had time to before.

'I know you want to see this Mr Liddle,' said Jane. 'But what else will we do in England?'

Amy was sitting on the edge of her bunk. She leant forward and clasped her hands round her knees.

'There's so much to see there, darling. So many wonderful buildings and so much history.'

Jane made a face. Old buildings and history weren't her idea of fun.

'Don't worry,' said Amy, catching her eye. 'I won't take you anywhere you don't want to go!'

'But who else do you know, Mum, apart from this Liddle man?'

'Well. I don't know anyone yet. But I intend to. We shall get to know people on the ship and perhaps they'll invite us to their homes. Then, I'd like to try to find some of your father's ancestors. A lot of them came from England.'

'But that was *years* ago!'

Amy plucked at the blanket on the bunk bed. 'Yes, I know. But old Will was interested in that sort of thing. His father, Amos, told him about his father's family in London and Will used to tell me about them. He'd intended to go to England himself, but of course he was always too busy with the hotel and then the war came and then he got sick. And when he was dying he made me promise him that one day I'd try to trace them.'

Jane sighed. It all sounded a bit of a muddle to her. She changed the subject. 'Tell me about the school I'm going to,' she said.

Amy brightened. 'It sounds perfect,' she said. 'You can board during the week and come home at weekends. That will give me time to do all the boring things I want to do and then we can do things that you and David want to do at the weekends.'

'But you've only booked us in for one term, haven't you?'

'Yes – for the moment, at least.'

'Mum! I don't want to stay away from Melbourne for too long.'

'You may love it over there, darling. Let's just see how things go, shall we?'

And with that, Jane had to be content.

# Bedford, April, present day

*When I got home this evening after seeing Keith, I couldn't stop shaking. Gran had waited up for me, and I wish she hadn't. She knew at once that something was wrong.*

*'What is it, Becky love? What's the matter? Is Mum worse?'*

*I shook my head. 'No, no, she's a bit better, I think. She made a sort of grunt and she opened her eyes, and Gran, she tried to smile when I said her name.'*

*Gran took my hand. 'That's fantastic, love. Fantastic!'*

*But she's a wily old bird, my gran. She wasn't going to be put off the scent. 'Something else is bothering you, dear, isn't it? Why don't you tell me about it?'*

*'It's nothing really. It's just that . . . well, I saw Keith this evening,' I said.*

*Gran's expression changed instantly. Perhaps she knows more than I think she does. 'He wasn't at the hospital, was he?'*

*I shook my head. 'Not at the hospital, but near the bus station.'*

*And then, suddenly, I started to shake again, and then I couldn't stop myself. I started to cry.*

*Gran put her arms round me and held me tight. She waited until I'd stopped, then she handed me a pile of tissues.*

*'I think you'd better tell me everything, Becky. There's something here that your grandad and I don't understand.'*

'But Mum wouldn't want me to,' I began. 'She didn't want you and Grandad upset.'

Gran put her hand under my chin and lifted it up until I was looking her straight in the eye.

'Your mum is unconscious in a hospital bed, Becky. If there's anything more I should know about that man, then you must tell me. I don't trust him. I never have. I was never happy when he and your mum were together.'

'But you never said!'

Gran sighed. 'Your mum's a grown woman. If I'd have given her my opinion, do you think it would have made a bit of difference?'

I shook my head and smiled weakly. 'Probably not.'

'No. Of course it wouldn't. So I kept my lip buttoned then and I'm glad I did. In the end she saw the light and sent him packing.'

I nodded, and she went on, 'So, what's he doing, lurking round here?'

I took a deep breath. 'He still wants her, Gran, and he knows he can't have her. I think he's set on revenge.'

Gran laughed. 'Don't be so dramatic, Becky!'

Suddenly I saw red. I was really angry with her. 'You've no idea,' I shouted. 'You've no idea what we've been through because of that man!'

'All right, dear, I'm sorry,' said Gran, evenly. 'But how can I know if you don't tell me?'

'Okay,' I mumbled. 'If you really want to know, I'll tell you.'

So, late into the night, I sat there in the kitchen and I told her. I told her everything. Well . . . almost everything.

Gran was silent for a while, then she said quietly, 'Do you think that Keith may have had something to do with Mum's accident?'

She's a mind-reader! It seemed so far-fetched, I'd said nothing about that.

'Yes,' I said slowly. 'Yes, I do. But I can't prove anything.'

'Show me the note you were talking about,' said Gran.

I got up and went to my room. I'd kept it with my underwear. It was crumpled and stained, but it was still quite readable. I took it down to Gran.

She put on her specs and then picked it up gingerly and, holding it away from her, read it out loud:

'I'm watching you. I know where you live. I know where you work. I know where Becky goes to school. Matt owes me £6,000. Get the money.'

Gran looked over the top of her specs at me and I shivered, suddenly. I couldn't help myself.

'Go to bed now, love,' said Gran, 'and try to get some sleep. Tomorrow we'll go to the police.'

'No, Gran, please! If he thinks we're involving the police, it will only make him worse!'

But she wasn't going to budge on this one.

'This is a police matter now, Becky. Let them deal with it.'

I went to bed then, but I couldn't sleep. She doesn't know him like we do. If he can force Mum off the road — or *whatever he did – then he could well start menacing Gran and Grandad – and me, too.*

*I know what will happen. The police will speak to him, he'll deny everything, he'll have an alibi for when the crash happened, the police will drop it and then he'll really make our lives a misery.*

# 4

## London, June 1947

They came in on the morning tide and the liner made its way slowly into the mouth of the River Thames and upriver towards the docks at Tilbury.

Jane, David and Amy were all at the rail, as were most of the other passengers. It was a grey, overcast day and there was a light breeze which rippled the water below.

Jane had heard all about the London Blitz and she knew that there'd been terrible damage done to London, but nothing prepared her for the gaping holes along the river frontage, the flattened buildings, the piles of rubble and the tall weeds growing in spaces where buildings had been.

'The river's *grey*,' said David.

'So's the River Yarra at home,' said Amy, cheerfully.

'Not as grey as this!'

David looked around him at the bombed-out warehouses. 'Is this London?'

Amy shook her head. 'Not really, it's the docks area. It's a long way up the river to the main city.'

'Hope it's better than this,' muttered David.

'London will be marvellous,' said Amy firmly.

Jane sneaked a glance at her. Nothing was going to dampen Amy's spirits. She was determined that this trip was going to be a success.

After what seemed an age and accompanied by a lot of shouting and banging and creaking, the ship finally docked, the gangway was lowered and the passengers started to disembark.

Jane watched as friends and families of other passengers rushed to greet them. She felt alone and strange.

They said goodbye to the various friends they'd made on board, who were all being met and soon vanished into the crowd, calling back with promises to meet up again soon.

The shipping company had made arrangements for some of the passengers, including Amy and her family, to take a bus into central London. At last, their trunks were located and packed on to the bus, and they started off on the long drive.

Frequently they caught glimpses of the river as they followed its course up towards the city. At first, most of the traffic consisted of lorries bringing goods down to the docks. They seldom saw private cars. But then, as the scene changed, they saw more. Some of them unfamiliar makes. David, who had been slumped grumpily in his seat, suddenly sat up and took more interest.

Then they were driving down the embankment, past some of the familiar landmarks which Amy had been trying to teach them about.

They had booked into a small hotel not far from Victoria Station. Amy felt that it would be good to be near a railway station, at least at first, so that they could travel around more easily.

They passed so many scenes of bombing, but they passed beautiful sights, too. The bridges over the Thames, Big Ben and the Houses of Parliament. Then suddenly they were swinging away from the river and up towards Victoria. Some of the houses they passed were very grand, but everywhere there were still the scars of war damage, with boarded-up windows and straggling weeds.

They were all hungry and tired by the time they reached their hotel. The man at reception who checked them in was pleasant enough and he found them porters to carry their trunks up to their rooms, but Amy's sharp eyes missed nothing and she could see that there was much room for improvement. The hotel's windows were grimy, the carpet old and dingy and the light over the stairs had not been replaced. But at least they did *have* electric light. She knew that many places in England (as in Australia) still hadn't got electricity.

They ate a dreary lunch in the almost empty dining-room.

'Tomorrow,' whispered Amy, 'we shall go and explore. We'll go and look at Buckingham Palace and at St Paul's Cathedral. We shall start to find our way around.'

David still looked glum, so Jane changed the subject. 'When are you going to meet Mr Liddle?' she asked.

'On Friday,' said Amy. 'He's coming to the hotel and we shall all go out to lunch.'

'When are we going to go to school?' asked David.

'Next week, dear. Then you'll only have a few weeks there before the summer holidays begin, so you won't feel so strange when you go back in September.'

Jane picked up on this immediately. 'So we're going to stay another term?' That would mean being in England through the winter.

'Maybe,' said Amy.

David and Jane exchanged glances. What had seemed like an adventure was starting to become all too real.

For the next few days, Amy took the children sightseeing. Jane knew that Amy was trying hard, but it was all so strange and they were so alone.

However, David did get excited when they watched the guard changing at Buckingham Palace and Jane liked walking in St James's Park and feeding the ducks and watching the uniformed nannies wheeling huge prams around.

The shops were exciting, too – much more interesting than those in Melbourne – even though there were still shortages after the war.

Friday came at last and Amy made the children dress in their best clothes for their lunch with Mr Liddle.

The fine weather had broken and summer showers pelted against the grimy windows of the hotel lounge as they waited nervously for this complete stranger who had known John. As they waited, Jane tried to recall her father, but things were getting less clear. She remembered a happy, smiling man who had hugged her and sometimes swung her round, who had played games with them when he wasn't too busy. And she remembered what he had looked like, because Amy had his picture with her all the time.

But he'd died five years ago and she and David hadn't seen him for over six years.

Try as she might, she couldn't really remember much about him; his image was fading.

Then, at last, through the lounge door, they saw Ernest Liddle arrive. He was wearing a bowler hat and holding a huge black umbrella over his head to protect him from the rain. As he reached the steps up to the hotel he let the umbrella down and shook it, then removed his hat and walked through the revolving doors into the reception area.

Amy rose immediately and went to greet him as he was announcing himself to the man behind the desk.

She smiled and put out her hand. 'Mr Liddle? How do you do. I'm Amy, John's wife.'

He turned slowly and looked at her, and then smiled a slow, wide smile.

Amy tried not to look shocked when she finally saw him properly. Even in the poor light of the hotel reception, she could see that he was painfully thin, that his hair was sparse and dry and that his complexion was papery and yellow.

But he shook her warmly by the hand and his grip was firm. 'I'm so glad to meet you after all this time,' he said quietly.

Amy led him into the lounge. David and Jane were standing there, looking awkward as she introduced them, but they were less able to hide their reaction to his appearance.

He smiled at them, sensing their unease. 'I look like an old skeleton, don't I, but there's nothing much I can do about it, I'm afraid. That's how the war has left me.'

Everyone relaxed then and before long they were all walking off down the street, huddled under Ernest's umbrella.

He took them to a restaurant that they would never have found for themselves. It was not far from the hotel but hidden in a back street. The food was simple but good and Amy and the children tucked in hungrily, but Ernest Liddle hardly touched what was on his plate.

After lunch, the rain had cleared, so they walked to St James's Park. The children strode ahead, but Amy walked with Ernest, realizing that he couldn't keep up. While they walked along she watched him carefully. He was obviously unwell, wheezing and stopping from time to time to catch his breath.

'Is it too much for you?' she asked gently. 'Shall I call a cab?'

He shook his head. 'No, it's good for me. If you don't mind walking slowly.'

When at last they reached the park, Amy and Ernest sat down on a bench and the children wandered off.

'Now,' said Amy. 'Please tell me everything.' Then she hesitated, suddenly realizing that this man had been through hell and might not want to bring back those memories. 'If . . . if you don't mind, that is,' she added.

He shook his head. 'Most of us don't talk about it much,' he said simply. 'But I know it's important to you.'

So, sitting there, with the afternoon sun glinting on the rain-soaked grass, he told her, slowly and simply, about that terrible time as a prisoner of war in Changi and then of his years working on the Burma railway. He spoke fondly of John, of their friendship and, eventually, of his death at the camp.

Amy bent her head and cried silently. Somehow, she didn't mind crying in front of this man who had seen raw emotions of every kind. At last, she calmed down and blew her nose.

'Thank you,' she said quietly. She put her hand on his arm. 'I hope you understand that I had to know.'

'Of course I understand,' he said.

For a while they were both silent, and then Amy spoke again. 'What about you?' she asked. 'What happened to you after John died?'

He sighed. 'I just went on working on the railroad,' he said simply. 'We had to. There was no choice.'

'And at the end of the war?'

'At the end, we were brought back to Changi.'

'The British were there then?'

He nodded. 'Our people were there and they were terribly shocked to see the state we were in. We came back in trucks. Many of the men couldn't even stand up after the journey south. All of us were desperately thin and many of us had contracted diseases.'

'Like you?' said Amy.

'Yes,' he said. 'I'm afraid my poor old chest will never recover.'

Amy said nothing, but she had a feeling that Ernest was telling her that he didn't have long to live.

'Anyway, what of you and your lovely children?' he asked. 'What are you planning to do in England?'

Amy shrugged. 'The most important thing was to see you and hear about John,' she said. 'But I do have other plans.'

'Yes?'

'Yes, I'd like to see something of the countryside

before the end of the summer. And I want to try to trace John's ancestors. His great-grandfather was born in London and there's probably still some family here. I'd like to find them if I can.'

'Do you know the name of his great-grandfather?'

'Yes,' said Amy. 'He was called Amos Harris and he worked as a harness-maker. He lived and worked in an area called East Smithfield and he left for Australia when he was eighteen. I believe he had a twin brother called Seth who was killed in an accident. And Seth was married and had a son so there should be some family still around.'

'You know a great deal, then,' said Ernest.

'Well, old Will, who was Amos's son, he helped run our hotel in Melbourne, and he used to tell me what Amos had told him.'

'It shouldn't be too difficult to find the family,' said Ernest. 'There are parish registers and the births and deaths registers at Somerset House.' He hesitated. 'I could help you, if you like.'

Amy clapped her hands together. 'Oh, I was hoping you'd say that,' she said. 'I'd be so grateful.'

Ernest smiled. 'I'd be happy to. Because of my health, I can't have a proper job now so it would be a good way to fill my time.'

'That's wonderful,' said Amy. 'We'll start as soon as the children are settled in school.'

Ernest smiled. 'I look forward to it,' he said. Then he

56

put his hand into the inside pocket of his jacket. 'And before I forget, let me give you this.'

Carefully, he pulled out a package wrapped in tissue paper and gave it to Amy.

Frowning, she unwrapped it, then gasped.

'John's gold watch and chain!' she said. But after turning it over in her hands a few times, she shook her head and tried to hand it back.

'John gave it to you,' she said. 'You should keep it.'

Ernest shook his head. 'No, it should go back to his family.' He pushed her hand away, then he turned the watch over as it lay in her palm, so that they could read the inscription on the back.

'*To my son, Charles Frobisher, on the occasion of his marriage. From his father. June 1830.*'

'Didn't you say that your mother was called Frobisher, before her marriage?'

Ernest nodded. 'Yes.'

Amy closed her hand over the watch. 'Then maybe this Charles Frobisher was some relation?'

Ernest shrugged. 'It's possible,' he said. 'There aren't that many people called Frobisher.'

'And maybe,' continued Amy, 'the watch was stolen from your relation by Amos's father. I believe there was some story about the watch being the reason why Amos's father was sent to Australia.'

'Who knows?' said Ernest.

'Who knows?' repeated Amy. And suddenly she felt

an overwhelming pity for this man whose life had been ruined by the war. For so long she had been bitter about John's death, but Ernest was experiencing a living death. He was still young and yet his life, she realized, was nearly over. If she had waited much longer to take this trip to London, she could have been too late.

She stood up. 'Thank you so much for everything,' she said quietly. 'Especially for telling me about John.'

'I hope it helped.'

She nodded. 'More than you can ever know.'

She called to the children, who were squatting by the pond, feeding the ducks. 'Jane, David, come on.'

Amy and the children said their goodbyes and set off back to their hotel, but Ernest stayed where he was, sitting on the park bench, his head full of scenes from the past.

At last he, too, stood up and walked slowly away in the opposite direction.

## Bedford, April, present day

*I had horrible nightmares last night. I dreamt that Keith was running after me and I couldn't move. I couldn't run away and he was coming closer and closer. Then I woke up with a start, sweating and shivering. My duvet was on the floor, so I must have been tossing and turning. By the early hours, I did, finally, sleep properly, and then, by the time I woke, it was mid-morning.*

I staggered down to the kitchen and Gran and Grandad were there, drinking coffee. Gran got straight to the point.

'We've phoned the police, Becky, and they're coming round soon, so get dressed quickly, dear.'

I opened my mouth to protest, but Gran cut me short. 'Hurry, dear. I'll bring some breakfast up to you to save time.'

I had only just managed to struggle into my jeans and take a bite of toast when the doorbell rang. I heard Grandad talking to someone and then footsteps coming through the house and into the kitchen.

My stomach was in knots. I remembered the awful time we'd had with the police when they'd thought that Matt had stolen the equipment from school. I so wished that Gran hadn't done this.

I sent Katie a text before I went downstairs. I wanted her to come over but I knew she'd gone off with her mum to visit some relations or something today.

So I took a deep breath and walked slowly down the stairs.

They all looked up when I came into the kitchen. There were two police officers — a man and a woman. The woman was young and pretty and she smiled at me. I didn't recognize her. Probably a good thing; she hadn't been around when Matt had disappeared so maybe she didn't know about all our baggage.

Gran fussed around and made them coffee and we all sat at the kitchen table.

'Tell them what you told me, Becky,' said Gran. 'Tell them about Keith, about the money, about seeing him – and show them the note, too.'

The policewoman glanced at her colleague. Then she turned to Gran and Grandad.

'I wonder if you'd mind if we talked to Becky on her own?' she asked.

Gran looked offended, but Grandad broke in. 'Come along, love,' he said firmly, taking Gran's arm.

'But . . .' she began.

'I'll be fine, Gran,' I said. I was secretly relieved that she and Grandad weren't going to stay and listen.

Once they'd gone, the police started asking me the usual questions. About Keith's relationship with Mum, with Matt, with me.

I tried to be fair. To tell them that at first Mum had really relied on him and it was only gradually that it had all started to go wrong. When she realized he was unbalanced. They seemed to know about Matt, so they'd obviously done their homework.

They were really nice and sympathetic and took lots of notes. When they went, the woman said, 'We'll make some enquiries, Becky, but I don't honestly know if we can help. He had every right to ask your brother to repay the money and, unless we have a witness who saw him near the scene of the accident, then I'm afraid no one can tell us what happened except your mother.'

I knew it! They're going to stir things up and it won't help us one bit!

Damn Gran. Damn her for interfering.

As soon as the police had gone I grabbed my bag and headed for the door.

'Where are you going?' asked Grandad, emerging from the lounge.

'Out,' I snapped. Then I slammed the door and went for a walk. I needed some air.

After a while, I calmed down. Suddenly I really wanted to see Mum, so I hopped on the bus that went to the hospital. I checked my mobile and found a message from Katie: 'Hang in there, babe. I'll be back later. Catch you then.' I smiled. I needed to talk it over with her.

Mum seemed restless when I saw her. She kept moving her head from side to side. I talked to the nurse, and asked whether this was a good sign.

'Well, I think her level of consciousness is improving all the time,' she said cautiously. 'She certainly seemed more aware when your uncle called earlier.'

My uncle?

The alarm bells started ringing. Mum doesn't have a brother and Dad's brother lives in Canada.

My stomach turned over. 'What uncle?' I asked, trying to sound normal.

'He called in earlier,' said the nurse. 'He sat with your mum for about an hour.'

Keith! It must have been Keith! Oh God. What shall I do?

# 5

## London, June 1947

Jane lay in her narrow bed in the dormitory. During the war, the whole school had been moved to the country, out of the way of the bombing, but now it had returned to London. Jane had been at the school for two weeks now, and she hated it. All the other girls knew each other and she felt a complete outsider. She didn't understand the rules, she didn't know how to play the games and she was either way behind in her lessons or way out in front. She was good at geography and not bad at science, but maths seemed to be taught quite differently and as for history... She'd never taken much notice of history at school in Melbourne because it all related to the old country – or the Mother Country, as England was called – and it was even worse here. She was expected to know about battles and kings and queens she'd never heard of and cared little or nothing about.

She sat up in bed and hugged her knees to her chest.

The blankets were thin and scratchy; that was another thing. She was supposed to make her bed each morning with *square* corners. She hadn't any idea what that meant but she soon learnt because some older girl came and inspected the beds each morning to see if they had been properly made.

Jane sighed and looked round her. All the other girls were asleep but Jane's head was too full of thoughts and she felt desperately homesick. Homesick for her life in Melbourne – her friends and her freedom – and she really missed her mum, too. A tear rolled down her cheek and she brushed it angrily away. If she kept her head down and tried to fit in, maybe it wouldn't be too bad.

There was one girl who had been kind to her. She was called Anne and she always seemed to find time to explain things to Jane.

It wasn't that the others were unkind, exactly, but they were always giggling and getting into huddles from which Jane was excluded. And she knew that they laughed at the way she spoke. The girls here spoke with such affected accents; people in Melbourne would have laughed at them, but here how you spoke seemed to determine what class you were. And this, apparently, was all-important!

Jane couldn't understand these English girls. Things like who you knew, what your father did, where you lived, all seemed terribly important to them. Things that Jane had never really thought about when she made her friends in Australia.

She wished with all her heart that Mum hadn't made her come to this school, even for the few weeks before the end of the summer term. But Mum was revitalized by this visit. She and Ernest Liddle had been poking around in records and apparently making some progress in finding Dad's family. Mum was really excited about it.

Jane had a feeling that Mum was here to stay. When she'd come to the school to take Jane back to the hotel for the weekend, she'd been so full of it. This was her adventure, her project, and she was going to sweep Jane and David along with her.

'Ernest says he can find us a flat to rent, so we don't have to live in that gloomy hotel any longer,' she'd said. 'And he knows a lot of people, too. We'll soon make friends, you'll see.'

That first weekend out of school was strange. David was restless and didn't want to be with them, Jane could tell. Unlike Jane, he'd immediately felt at home at his new school. He excelled at sports – always had – and that made him instantly popular. He talked non-stop about this boy or the other and whether he could get into the first eleven for some match. It was all gibberish to Jane, although Amy tried to take an interest and was obviously pleased that he'd settled in so well.

Jane felt that, for the first time in their lives, she and

David were drifting apart. They'd always been so close but now they were beginning to go their separate ways.

It was with a heavy heart that she'd gone back to school at the beginning of this week and she couldn't wait until the end of term.

As she sat there, feeling miserable and empty, someone stirred on the other side of the room. Jane was about to lie down again, not wanting to draw attention to herself, when she realized that it was Anne who was looking across at her. Hauling on her dressing-gown, Anne left her bed and padded quickly over to Jane.

She perched on the end of Jane's bed. 'It will get better, Jane,' she whispered. 'It's not such a bad place and you'll soon get used to it.'

Jane sniffed, trying hard not to start crying again. It was worse when someone was being nice to her. 'Sorry,' she said.

'What for?' said Anne. 'We all get homesick sometimes and you're much further from your home than the rest of us.'

'It just seems so strange,' said Jane. 'I don't fit in here and I don't understand things.'

'You will,' said Anne. 'In time, you will.' Then she asked, 'Your father died in the war, didn't he?'

Jane nodded. Then she said, 'What about you? Did you lose anyone?'

Anne picked a loose thread from the blanket. 'Yes,' she said quietly. 'My mother was killed in the Blitz. She was driving an ambulance.'

'Your mother!'

Anne nodded. 'Strange, isn't it? My father fought in the war and came back alive but my mother was killed here in London.'

Suddenly, Jane felt ashamed. Losing a father whom she hardly remembered was bad enough. But to lose your *mother*!

She squeezed Anne's hand. 'I'm so sorry,' she whispered.

Anne nodded silently. 'I think of her a lot – and I know Father does. He tries so hard but he can't do everything she did for us.' She sighed. 'We have a housekeeper, but it's not the same.'

They were silent for a while, then Jane said, hesitantly, 'When we're settled in this new flat, would you be allowed to come out and visit us for the weekend?'

'I'd like that,' said Anne.

They chatted a bit more, then Anne went back to her own bed and Jane lay down in hers. Just that brief talk had made her feel much better and it wasn't long before she drifted off and slept soundly for the rest of the night.

The following weekend, Amy arrived at Jane's school in a flurry of excitement. David was already with her, looking awkward with all the girls about the place, and Amy had so much to tell them both that Jane couldn't get a word in edgeways.

'Ernest has borrowed a car,' she said, leading Jane towards it. 'And we are to move into the flat this morning. And guess what?'

'What?'

'We've found out about Dad's family and we're going to visit the place where your great-great-grandfather Amos worked!'

Ernest was standing by the car, smiling. Jane was shocked. He looked even more ill than before. Could he really spend the day helping them move and then driving them on some wild goose chase to see where a long-dead relation of Dad's used to work?

David yawned. Bored at the prospect of what lay ahead.

'Come on,' said Amy. 'Back to the hotel to collect our bags.'

Jane noticed that Ernest didn't offer to carry any of their bags and she was relieved. But he organized for porters at the hotel to load the heavy stuff into the car and, Jane noticed, he tipped them generously, too.

The flat was some way from Victoria, just off Baker Street in the West End, in a quiet leafy square called Montagu Square.

'It's not very fashionable,' said Ernest, smiling, 'but the rent's reasonable and it's quite central.'

Amy put her hand on his arm. 'It's wonderful,' she said. Then she turned to the twins. 'Now you two must help me get the luggage up these stairs,' she said firmly.

It was hard work heaving their possessions up three flights of stairs, but when Amy turned the key in the lock and flung open the door, Jane couldn't help clapping her hands with excitement.

The sun streamed through the huge windows of the main room, which overlooked the square. It was big and airy and had high moulded ceilings. There were three bedrooms, a good-sized bathroom and a modern kitchen with lino on the floor, an electric cooker and lots of cupboards.

Jane flung her arms round Amy's neck. 'Oh, Mum, it's lovely!'

Amy was flushed with pleasure. 'I'm so pleased you like it. But you have Ernest to thank. He found it for us.'

Jane turned to Ernest, who had taken a long time to climb the stairs and was standing behind them, holding on to the bannister, fighting for breath.

'It's lovely, Mr Liddle,' she said.

Ernest Liddle smiled, then he sat down quietly in a chair in the corner of the room.

Amy had brought some food and they had a picnic in their new kitchen. Jane hadn't seen her mother look so happy for a long time.

After lunch, they unpacked their things while Ernest

rested, and the flat began to take on something of their personalities.

'What do you think?' said Jane to David.

'Yeah. It's nice.'

Amy and Jane exchanged glances. This was high praise from David.

'We'll have a lot of fun here, I promise,' said Amy. 'And at last I shall be able to cook again.'

Ernest looked up from his chair. 'You'll hire a cook, won't you? And someone to clean?'

Amy shrugged. 'You forget, Ernest,' she said gently. 'I'm used to cooking and cleaning. I enjoy it.'

After lunch, they went down to the square and piled into the big old car. Amy leant forward and said quietly to Ernest, 'Are you sure you feel up to this?'

For answer, he started the engine and they were soon heading back down to the river and out to the east.

'Don't get used to this,' said Amy to the twins. 'It'll be back to the buses and tubes tomorrow. Ernest has only borrowed the car for the day.'

They stopped a few times. Ernest made a show of looking at the map but Jane was sure that he needed to stop to ease his painful breathing. The traffic wasn't heavy and they made good progress.

As they drove again along the embankment, beside the River Thames, Jane marvelled at how much more appealing it looked in the sunshine. Then as they continued east they came to Tower Bridge, which had opened in the middle to let through a tall ship. Then, almost immediately, they were turning away from the river and up to East Smithfield.

They fell silent as they drove down the big wide road. The bombing damage here was terrible.

'It's very near the docks,' said Ernest.

'Is that why it's so badly bombed?' asked David.

Ernest nodded.

They peered at the numbers – such numbers as were left.

'It must be round here,' said Amy, but her voice was flat with disappointment.

Ernest parked the car and they all got out. They stared round at the huge untidy gaps where there had once been businesses or houses. Amy walked over to one of the empty spaces, where now there was nothing but rubble and weeds.

'I think it would have been about here,' she said quietly, consulting the address she had written down on a piece of paper.

'Do you think the people were inside when the bomb fell?' asked David.

Ernest shrugged. 'If they were lucky, they would have heard the air-raid warning and gone to a shelter,' he said.

Amy bent her head. She was very quiet.

'We could ask, couldn't we?' said Jane. 'See if anyone round here knows what happened?'

Amy looked up. 'Yes, yes, of course we could.'

Nervously, they went to the nearest place which seemed to have signs of life. It was — or had been — some sort of warehouse, but it too had been badly damaged, and most of the windows were still boarded up. They found a man wheeling big boxes out to the back and asked him if he knew anything about the building where the harness-maker had once been.

He shook his head, but then, seeing Amy's disappointment, he said, 'There's Tom. 'E's bin round 'ere for ever. Come with me and we'll see if 'e can remember.'

Jane thought that Tom looked about a hundred. He was sitting on a low wall at the back of the building, his face tipped up towards the sunshine. He was smoking a pipe which, to Jane, had a vile smell, and at first he didn't seem too pleased to be disturbed.

'Nah,' he said. 'There weren't no 'arness-maker there. Not that I know of. Most of the leather workers were further south — off Tower Bridge Road.'

'It was a long time ago,' said Amy, 'but I just thought maybe when you were a boy . . .' She trailed off.

Tom scratched his head with his free hand. 'Not so much call for 'arness-makers these days,' he said. 'All motor cars now.'

Jane turned to Amy. 'Did you find out anything else about Dad's people?'

Amy frowned. 'Only what old Will told me. I think

71

he said there was a dressmaking business, too, but I couldn't find any record of that.'

Tom took his pipe out of his mouth. 'Dressmaking, you say?'

Amy nodded.

'Now, I maybe could 'elp you there,' he said. 'There was a fine dressmaker lived along here, in my grandfather's time. Employed all these girls. I remember going there as a boy to help sweep the floor and that.' He smiled thoughtfully. 'Pretty lasses they were, too.'

'What happened to the business?' asked Amy.

Tom shrugged. 'Moved up west. Got too grand for down 'ere.'

'You don't remember where it moved to?'

Tom shook his head. 'But I remember its name,' he said suddenly. 'It were called Abigail's Gowns. Bin going for years.'

'Abigail's Gowns,' repeated Amy, looking at Ernest.

'We should be able to find records of the business now we know its name,' he said.

Amy smiled at him. 'Yes. Yes, we'll start looking next week,' she said.

She was quiet on the drive back to Montagu Square, even when Ernest diverted and drove them down Oxford Street with all its big shops.

When they reached the flat, Ernest rested for a while and then left them. They leant out of the big windows and waved as he started the car and headed off.

'He looks so ill, Mum,' said Jane.

Amy nodded. 'He is, dear.'

For the rest of the weekend they explored their new area and worked out how to get to other places they wanted to see. And they made some plans for the holidays, too.

'Do you think you'll ever find these relations of Dad's?' asked David.

'I don't see why not,' said Amy. 'I'm not going to give up easily.'

On Sunday, when it was time for David and Jane to return to their schools, Jane said suddenly, 'Mum, could I bring a friend next weekend – if she wants to come?'

Amy looked pleased. 'Yes, of course, dear. I'll talk to the people at the school and find out if that's allowed. There are so many rules here!'

David looked glum. It was bad enough trailing round after Mum and Jane, when he'd prefer to be at school, but another girl was the last straw!

'Er . . . could I stay at school next weekend? It's just that there's a match on Saturday I really want to see.'

Amy hesitated. 'Well, I'll have to ask your teachers,' she said. 'I'd arranged for you to come home each weekend.'

'Oh please, Mum!'

'I'll see what I can do.'

★  ★  ★

Jane went back to school more happily after the weekend. At last she had somewhere she could call home, at least for the time being. While Amy waited in the school office, Jane went off to find Anne. Shyly, she asked if she'd like to come to the flat next weekend.

Anne smiled broadly. 'That would be wonderful,' she said. 'It would be good to get out of this place.' She really seemed pleased.

Jane took her to meet Amy and it was all arranged.

Suddenly, the school, the rules, the lessons, seemed easier to bear. It was a glorious sunny week and Jane's gloom lifted as the girls could spend more time outside and Jane could lift her face to the sky in the way she had always done in Melbourne.

The other girls seemed less strange now, less threatening. Perhaps another term at this place wouldn't be so bad after all.

During the week, Amy telephoned the school and Jane was called down to the office to take the call. This was highly unusual and Jane could sense the disapproval of the headmistress as she indicated the big black telephone on the desk.

Jane was suddenly fearful. Why should Mum ring in the middle of the week? Something bad must have happened.

'Jane, is that you?' Her voice sounded strained.

'Mum? What's the matter?'

'It's Ernest, dear. He's had to go into hospital.'

'Is he very bad?'

There was a pause. 'Yes, I'm afraid he is.' Then she continued, 'I feel I must be at the hospital, Jane . . . to . . . well, to say goodbye to him. He's done so much for us . . . and for Dad. So I may be at the hospital a lot over the weekend.'

'Do you still want us to come?'

'Oh yes, dear. You come, and your friend, if you still want to. But I won't be able to take you round. It may be very dull for you.'

'We'll be okay, Mum. Don't worry.'

'Are you sure, dear?'

'Sure.'

'Then I'll pick you up on Saturday.'

Jane felt sad about Ernest, but she couldn't help being excited, too. The prospect of spending two days without much supervision, and with a good friend, was liberating. Unusual, too. From what she'd heard from the other girls, she already had much more freedom than they did at their homes.

When Amy picked them up on Saturday she took Jane and Anne straight to the flat.

'Oh, it's lovely!' said Anne. 'You are lucky.'

'Where do you live, dear?' asked Amy.

'We live out in the country, in Wiltshire,' said Anne. 'The school moved there during the war and that's when I started going to it. Then when it moved back to London, I came, too.'

'Jane's told me about your mother, dear. I'm so sorry. War's a beastly business.'

Amy had cooked them a special lunch and Anne ate every scrap.

'You didn't tell me your mum could cook!' said Anne.

Jane laughed. 'This is nothing, is it, Mum?' Then she turned to Anne. 'She used to do the food for a whole hotel full of people in Melbourne.'

Anne stared. '*You* did the cooking? Didn't you have a cook?'

Amy smiled. 'We had cooks, yes, but during the war it was difficult to keep staff, so I did a lot of the cooking.'

'I wish our housekeeper could cook,' sighed Anne. 'I mean cook really nice food, like this.'

'I'm glad you like it.'

After the meal, Amy said she must go to the hospital.

'Is he very bad?' asked Jane.

Amy nodded. 'I'm afraid so.' She hesitated. 'He has a lot of visitors – family and friends – but he keeps asking for me, so I feel I should try to be there as much as possible.' She hesitated. 'He hasn't got long.'

Jane didn't know what to say, so she changed the subject. 'Have you found out any more about Dad's family?'

Amy nodded. 'Well, yes, I have. I've got quite a few more leads – some addresses and so on – but what with Ernest being so ill . . .' She trailed off. Then she stood up and started clearing the dishes.

'We'll do this, Mum,' said Jane. 'You get off to the hospital.'

After Amy had left, Jane and Anne did the dishes.

'Before the war, girls like us were never allowed into the kitchen,' said Anne.

Jane stared at her. 'Why ever not?'

Anne shrugged. 'It was the place for the cook and the servants,' she said. Then, seeing Jane's horrified face, she laughed. 'But things have changed since the war,' she said. 'People don't have many servants now so we're all having to learn to do things for ourselves.'

Jane was quiet for a while, remembering her own relationship with their staff at the hotel in Melbourne. She'd never thought of them as servants; they were her friends. How different it all was over here.

'Who's your mother trying to trace?' asked Anne, breaking the silence.

Jane smiled. 'Oh, she's got the bit between her teeth. She's determined to trace my father's English ancestors.' She shrugged. 'I don't know what she thinks will happen when she does find them, but she's determined. It's a sort of quest.'

'Why don't we help her, then?'

'What, go looking for them ourselves?'

Anne nodded. 'It would be something to do tomorrow. Your mother's friend is dying and she's going to be at the hospital all the time. Come on, say you will. It will be fun!'

It was late when Amy returned that evening, but the girls were still up, chatting away.

Amy looked tired and sad. 'He's so weak,' she said. 'And every breath he takes is a struggle.' She sighed. 'He can't last much longer.'

'Mum,' said Jane gently. 'Me and Anne thought we could carry on looking for Dad's people if you'd let us – tomorrow, while you're at the hospital?'

Amy looked up, surprised. 'I thought you weren't really interested in all that.'

Jane shrugged. 'I don't know enough about them, but you're keen to find them, aren't you, Mum?'

Amy smiled and passed her hand over her brow. 'It's for old Will, really. I'm doing it for him – and for myself. And for Dad, too.'

'Will ran the hotel in Melbourne,' explained Jane to Anne. 'His father and grandfather started it.'

'Will had never been to England,' said Amy, 'though he'd always hoped to, but the war came and John went off to fight, so Will couldn't leave Melbourne.'

Amy shifted in her seat. 'His father, Amos, had come out from England when he was only eighteen. Amos's own father had left his mother and his twin brother and gone to Australia. Everyone believed that he'd been drowned when the ship sank, but Amos had this strong feeling that his father was still alive, so he went to Australia to see if he could find him.'

'And did he?' asked Anne.

'Yes, after two years of searching, he did find him. He'd changed his name to Henry Jones and had a new family – a wife called Molly and a daughter called Harriet – but he never denied that Amos was his son.'

'Amos must have been very angry with him for deserting them,' said Jane.

'Yes, according to Will, it took Amos a long time to forgive his father, but in the end they became good friends and business partners.'

'But what about the family back in England? Did Amos ever tell them he'd found his father?'

Amy shook her head. 'No. He never told them. He didn't want to hurt them.' Then she went on, slowly. 'I've never told you this before, Jane, but Will was illegitimate. His mother was a young girl Amos knew up in Gippsland, the daughter of one of the miners there.'

Anne blushed and looked shocked, but Jane was fascinated. 'Goodness! So, what happened to Will's mother?'

'She died giving birth to Will. Your great-great-grandfather Amos paid for Will to be cared for by the girl's father, but he got sick and he took Will back to Amos. It was a bad time for your great-great-grandmother, Flo. She had just lost their first baby. But she took Will in and treated him as her own.'

She smiled. 'And the rest you know. Will and his aunt Harriet ran the hotel for years after Amos died and they made a real success of it.'

'What a story!' said Anne.

'So you can understand why Will had always wanted to know about his other family. The family in England who he had never met.'

'And he told you what he knew?'

Amy sighed. 'Yes, when John was away at the war, we often used to talk about it. And as he got older and it was less and less likely that he would ever get to England, he made me promise to try to find his other family.'

'Well, we can help you,' said Anne firmly. 'Tell us what you've found out already.'

Then, although it was late, Amy took out papers and lists from her desk and together the three of them pored over them.

'We've come to a dead end on the harness-making business,' she said. 'But Amos's aunt Abbie was a dressmaker – a very successful one, by all accounts.'

'Abbie – Abigail's Gowns!' said Jane.

'Yes. It seems that Abigail's Gowns went on for years after Abbie's death. Amos's mother, Sarah, and his sister-in-law – the widow of Seth, Amos's twin brother – were involved and so was Abbie's daughter, Victoria. Then it must have gone on down the family, but we don't know who Victoria married or whether other members of the family were in it, so the trail's gone cold.'

'Does Abigail's Gowns still exist?' asked Anne.

'No, it seems to have closed down just before the war,' said Amy. She rummaged among her papers, drew out a sheet and looked at it carefully. 'Here we are. It was in Soho Square, wherever that is.'

Anne was about to speak, but thought better of it.

'Where's that?' asked Jane.

Amy got the map and the two of them found it.

'It's not that far from here,' said Jane. 'We could go there tomorrow!'

Amy looked concerned. 'Are you sure, dear? You are only thirteen. I'm not sure I should let you travel round a big city on your own.'

'There are two of us,' said Jane, grinning at Anne. 'We'll be fine. And I won't get lost if Anne's with me.'

'Well . . .'

'Oh, come on, Mum. You can trust us.'

Amy smiled. 'All right then. Just so long as you are very careful and sensible. And make sure you are back here by six o'clock.'

They all went to bed then, but as Jane and Anne were undressing, Anne said, 'Soho's a bad place, Jane.'

Jane's eyes widened. 'What sort of bad?'

Anne looked uncomfortable. 'Lots of low-life,' she said primly. 'And . . . and bad women.'

Jane grinned. 'Hey, it'll be an adventure then!'

# 6

## Bedford, April, present day

*A*s soon as I left the hospital I phoned Katie and we
arranged to meet up in a coffee shop in town when she
got back. I couldn't face going back to the house so I mooched
around the shops. The time dragged.

In the end, I phoned Matt, too. I just got the voicemail, as
I knew I would, and I tried not to sound panicky. 'Please
phone back, Matt,' I said. 'Keith's been to see Mum and I
don't know what to do.'

Poor Matt. He's had enough of Keith and his bully-boy
tactics to last him a lifetime. I really didn't want to bother him
now he's so happy and so busy, but he needs to know what's
happening.

Katie arrived at the coffee shop, out of breath from running.

'I hope it's important, Becks,' she said. 'I got here as quick
as I could.'

So I told her.

She nodded slowly. 'Yep. I guess that's important.' Then
she took a sip of coffee. 'So, what are we going to do?'

I grinned. The first time I'd smiled all day. It was so good to hear her say 'we'. I told her about Gran getting the police round.

'Bet he's been watching your house, petal,' said Katie. 'Maybe that wasn't such a smart move.'

'Tell me about it,' I said.

'D'you think the police have been to see him?' said Katie.

I shrugged. 'I hope not. If they do, it will make him even angrier.'

We didn't say anything for a bit. I know Katie so well and I know that when she frowns and bites her lip it means she's thinking.

'How about,' she said at last, 'we take our books to the park opposite the hospital tomorrow and revise there? There's a shelter if we get cold – or wet.'

I knew at once what she was thinking. 'What, stake out the hospital? Watch for him to come again?'

'Yep. Then follow him, so we know where he's living.'

'P'raps he's not living here, just visiting? His business is somewhere up north.'

Katie shook her head. 'Maybe it is. But he wants to be near your mum and I'll bet my life that he's staying around here at the moment.'

I was unsure. 'Yeah, but even if we do find out where he's staying,' I said, 'what do we do then?'

Katie thought for a while. 'We'll think of something,' she said firmly.

The next day I told Gran that I'd go to the hospital first and then I'd spend the rest of the day with Katie, revising.

All absolutely true.

It was quite a nice day, thank goodness. Bright and breezy, so it wasn't too bad in the shelter, and Katie was right – it gave us a good view of the hospital entrance. We could see who went in and who came out. Once or twice some boys gave us a bit of trouble but they were only larking about and they soon lost interest. And we even got some work done. At lunch-time we ate the stuff we'd sneaked out from our homes, but we really wanted a hot drink so I went off to get one. I suppose I was gone about ten minutes.

When I got back, Katie was pacing up and down outside the shelter.

'What's up?' I said, handing her a drink.

She put both hands round the cup to warm them.

'He's been,' she said quietly. 'He's in the hospital now.'

Suddenly I saw red. I dumped my drink on the bench and ran towards the hospital entrance.

How dare he? I'd front up to him and accuse him of all the dreadful things he'd done to our family. How dare he!

But Katie was too quick for me. She raced after me, still clutching her drink, slurping it everywhere, and grabbed me.

'Don't be such an idiot, Becky,' she said. 'If you go crashing in there, you'll mess up everything.'

'He'll upset Mum,' I yelled. I began to cry – tears of pent-up fury and frustration.

I tried to break away from Katie but she held on tight. I

84

gave a twist, but that sent the rest of her hot chocolate flying out of her hand and all the way down my front.

We stood there looking at the brown stain seeping into my jacket and T-shirt, then we both started laughing.

'Come on, let's go back to the shelter and wait,' said Katie.

I smiled. 'I suppose you want to share my drink,' I said.

It was another half-hour before Keith came out again. Just the sight of him sent prickles of fear and hatred through me.

Katie started packing up the books into her backpack and mine. Keith was walking away fast.

'Come on,' she said. 'Time to go.'

But I was nervous. 'Do you really think we should?' I said.

Katie didn't answer. She just gave me a withering look and started off.

I trailed after her, feeling sick.


## London, June 1947

Jane and Anne finally got away from the flat mid-morning. Amy didn't really want them to go and needed all sorts of promises from them about taking care and being back early, but at last they were free and they ran up the road towards Baker Street, laughing and chatting. They'd studied the map carefully and decided it would be quicker to walk.

'It will only take about half an hour,' said Anne. 'And anyway, it's more fun.'

They headed over Baker Street and down New Cavendish Street, then turned right towards Oxford Street.

'You sure you know where you're going?' said Jane. 'It's taking ages.'

'No it's not,' said Anne. 'And yes, I do know where we're going.'

All round them they could hear the sound of bells, summoning people to church.

'It feels funny not to be going to church on a Sunday,' said Anne.

'Do you go every Sunday at school?'

Anne nodded. 'Without fail. We all line up in our hats and coats and gloves, then we walk to church two by two.'

On the other side of Oxford Street, the roads became smaller and the girls threaded their way through twists and turns in the route. Anne read out each street name as they went along.

'Bentinck Street, Noel Street, Wardour Street, Carlisle Street.'

At last they came into Soho Square.

'It's lovely,' said Jane. 'I thought you said it was a bad area.'

'Well, I've never actually been here before, but Soho's got a bad reputation,' said Anne, looking about her fearfully.

Jane shrugged. 'Everything looks very quiet to me,' she said.

'That's probably because it's Sunday,' said Anne, darkly.

Jane stopped in her tracks. 'We should have thought,' she said, stamping her foot in frustration. 'Nothing will be open. There'll be no one around to ask!'

'Well, let's see where this famous Abigail's Gowns was, anyway,' said Anne.

Jane drew out a scrap of paper from her pocket. 'The records said it was at 10–12 Soho Square,' she said, frowning.

'There,' said Anne, pointing over to the other side of the square.

'Doesn't look much like a dress shop now,' said Anne, as they approached the big old building.

They climbed the front steps and looked at the shiny brass notice screwed to the door.

'Insurance,' said Anne, dully.

'Sounds pretty boring,' said Jane. 'What shall we do now?'

They sat down on the steps in the sunshine.

'We've come all this way for nothing,' said Jane, hugging her knees.

'Well, we know where it *was*,' said Anne, trying to be cheerful.

'I'm fed up with the whole thing,' said Jane. 'I can't understand why Mum wants to track these people down anyway. She doesn't know any of them and I don't expect they'll want to see us.'

'I think it would mean a lot to her,' said Anne quietly.

Jane sighed. 'I suppose so.'

Anne picked at a thread in her cardigan. 'You know, you're lucky, Jane.'

'Why?'

Anne shrugged. 'It's hard to explain,' she said. 'You're different . . .'

'You're telling me!'

'No, I mean nicely different. You don't worry about your place in society, like most of us do.'

Jane hooted with laughter. 'Of course I don't. And what does it matter, anyway?' she said.

'You're right. It shouldn't matter. But it does. It matters a lot to people in this country. You are stuck with who you are, who your parents are, where you fit in society. You're labelled, from birth.'

'Do *you* think it's important, Anne?'

Anne shook her head. 'I always used to, but since I met you – and your mother – I'm not so sure any more.' She went on, 'She's lovely, your mother. I've never met anyone like her. She speaks to you as if you are another adult. No one's ever done that to me before.'

Jane looked up, surprised. 'She's just my mother, Anne. She's always been like that. But she's not unusual. Not for an Australian.'

Anne sighed. 'I wish I could go to Australia, then.'

'Perhaps you will one day.'

There were a few people walking through the square, but they all looked purposeful and the girls didn't dare approach them.

'Let's eat our sandwiches in that little garden,' said Jane, pointing to the middle of the square, 'then we can decide what to do with the rest of the day.'

'Oh, I don't think we're allowed . . .' began Anne.

Jane propelled her forward. 'Don't be such a silly goose. What harm would we do?'

Anne looked furtive as they opened the gate and went into the garden, then sat down on a bench.

'There,' said Jane. 'That's nice, isn't it?'

Anne still looked uneasy. 'I suppose so,' she said, uncertainly, 'but I'm sure there're rules.'

'Pooh! Rules!'

But sitting there with the strong summer sun streaming on to them through the gaps in the leaves, Anne started to relax.

They'd almost finished, when suddenly Jane saw something. She stiffened.

'Look!' she said. 'Someone's going up the steps to the building!'

Anne twisted round. 'They look like cleaners,' she said.

'Quick,' said Jane, scattering the rest of their picnic as she ran out of the garden and across the road.

She arrived at the building just as two women, both wearing overalls and with their hair tied up in scarves, were unlocking the front door.

'Excuse me!' said Jane, breathlessly, pounding up the steps behind them.

Both the women jumped. Jane noticed that one had a cigarette hanging out of the side of her mouth.

'Cor blimey,' she spluttered, 'you didn't 'arf give us a turn, love!'

Jane grinned. 'Sorry,' she said.

'We thought you were going to 'ave a right go at us for coming today instead of yesterday,' said the other. 'By rights, we shouldn't be cleaning on a Sunday but my Alf's got this . . .'

Jane wasn't listening. 'No, nothing like that,' she said, smiling. 'I . . . well, I wanted to know about Abigail's Gowns.'

One of the women turned to the other. 'Don't she talk funny,' she said, giggling.

Anne had arrived by this time. 'She's from Australia,' she explained.

'Australia!' said one of the women. 'Well I never.'

'And she's trying to find out about her family, who used to run Abigail's Gowns.'

Jane looked at the women, hopefully. Was it her imagination, or did they exchange a warning glance?

'Abigail's Gowns,' said one, slowly.

'Yes,' said Jane. 'It used to be here, didn't it? Before the insurance people came?'

The woman with the cigarette took it out of her mouth, stubbed it out on the side of the wall and then carefully put the remains in the pocket of her overall.

'Yeah, dear. It did.'

'Do you know what happened? Did it close down? Did it move somewhere else?'

The other woman suddenly burst out, 'Close down! I'll say it closed down. That bastard ran it into the ground and fired all the workers. I should know. I used to work here! It were a nice little family business until he stuck his evil fingers in it.'

'Florrie!' said the other woman. 'Leave it alone. You'll only upset yerself.'

'Who?' asked Jane, intrigued. 'Who was running it?'

'Yer don't want to know about all that,' said the woman with the cigarette, firmly. ''E were a slippery begger and he ruined a good little business.'

'What was his name?' asked Jane.

The same woman answered her. 'Leave it be, dear. Believe me, you want nawt to do with the likes of 'im.' She opened the front door and went inside.

'Come on, Florrie, we best get to work.'

'But he might be our relative,' said Jane, as the door was closing.

Florrie followed her friend, but Jane grabbed her sleeve. 'Please tell me his name at least,' she said.

Florrie folded her arms and looked her straight in the eye. 'It won't do you no good,' she said. 'But I'll tell you 'is name. It's Peter Daniels.' Then she spat on the ground and wiped her hand over her mouth.

'Where is he now? And was he a member of the family that owned it?'

''E's still somewhere around here, God rot 'im. 'E won't move from Soho. 'E's got 'is fingers in that many pies round 'ere.'

'Was he a member of the family?' Jane persisted.

Florrie nodded. 'Trampled over 'em all,' she said. 'Didn't care about no one but 'imself. Made money by squeezing the poor workers, then 'e closed the place down when he'd taken everything he could from it. 'E drove 'is poor mother to an early death.'

She shook Jane's arm off her and went inside, but as she was closing the door behind her she added, 'If you find the bastard, you punch 'is face in for me, will you?'

The door banged shut and Jane and Anne looked at each other.

'Well!' said Anne.

'Peter Daniels,' said Jane. 'He sounds a character!'

Anne looked horrified. 'A *character*! A criminal more like!'

'Interesting,' said Jane. 'I bet we could find him if we tried.'

'Jane, you're not seriously going to try to find a man like that?'

Jane grinned. 'Mum wants to track down the family, doesn't she?'

'I thought you said you weren't that interested.'

Jane took Anne's arm. 'Ah, but this Peter Daniels fellow sounds like a scoundrel. I'd like to know if we've got someone like *that* in the family.'

'Your mother would never let you go looking for someone bad like that, would she?'

'We don't have to tell her *everything* about him, do we?'

'We?'

'You *are* going to help me, aren't you?'

'Well . . .'

'See, if we find him, he might have other family around. Like you said,' she said, grinning, 'we owe it to Mum, don't we? We owe it to her to find out all we can.'

Anne laughed. 'I've never met anyone who could twist things around like you can,' she said.

They went back to the garden in the square and ate the rest of their picnic.

'Come on, Anne,' said Jane, when they'd finished.

'Come on where?'

'We can't waste the rest of the day. We're going to do some detective work!'

'How? What do you mean?'

'We'll start with the phone directory,' said Jane firmly, and she set off full of purpose, with Anne trailing behind her.

At the first red phone box they came to, Jane stopped, pulled open the heavy door and went inside. Anne followed and they squeezed in together. The phone box stank of cigarette smoke and sweat. Anne almost gagged as she breathed in the fetid fumes.

'It stinks in here,' she said, pinching her nose and breathing through her mouth.

Jane made a face. 'We'll get out as soon as we can,' she said.

There were two big London directories, both chained to the wall and both grimy and torn with overuse.

Jane started looking under the Ds.

'There are masses of P Danielses here,' she said. 'It must be a common name.'

'Read out the street names,' said Anne. 'And I'll check them on the map and see if any are round here.'

It took ages, but at last they found three P Danielses with addresses in Soho. One in Old Compton Street, one in Dean Street and one in Wardour Street.

'They're all close by,' said Jane, looking over Anne's

shoulder as she pored over the map. 'Which shall we try first?'

'Oh, Jane, do you really think . . .'

'Come on! We've got this far. It's an adventure.'

Anne frowned. Her stomach felt tense. She wasn't sure that this was the sort of adventure she wanted to be part of.

'Which is nearest?' said Jane.

'Er . . . Dean Street's just round the corner.'

Jane put her finger on the place. 'We'll go there first, then walk down to Old Compton Street and then across to Wardour Street.'

As they walked down Dean Street, there was a change in the feel of the place. Soho Square had seemed respectable enough, but even Jane could sense that two well-dressed young girls looked out of place, walking through a sleazy area on a Sunday, and they certainly attracted attention. Occasionally people would stare openly at them.

'I'm frightened, Jane,' said Anne.

'Don't be a baby. Nothing's going to happen to us,' said Jane, sounding more confident than she really was.

'I think we're being followed,' said Anne, looking anxiously over her shoulder. And, indeed, there was a man with slicked-back hair and a dark suit walking behind them.

'Don't be silly,' said Jane firmly. Then, 'What was the number in Dean Street?'

'It's over there,' said Anne, pointing nervously.

It was a tall thin building squeezed between two shuttered shops. There didn't seem to be a knocker or a bell, so before she could have second thoughts, Jane banged loudly on the door.

Nothing happened.

'Let's go,' whispered Anne, looking round anxiously. The man with the slicked-back hair had disappeared, but she still felt uneasy.

Jane knocked again. Still no answer.

She sighed. Anne was already walking away and Jane turned to follow her when, quite suddenly, the door opened and a sleepy-looking woman stood there, her arms folded. There were still traces of heavy make-up on her face. She looked at the girls with suspicion.

'What d'yer want?'

Suddenly Jane felt incredibly stupid. 'I'm looking for someone called Peter Daniels,' she said at last, her voice squeaky.

The woman's face relaxed then. 'You've come to the wrong place, love,' she said, quite kindly. 'There's no Peter Daniels 'ere.'

'It said P Daniels in the phone books,' said Jane, weakly.

The woman coughed. 'Yeah, that's me, dear. Prudence Daniels. Prudence by name, prudent by nature. That's what I say.' Then she laughed loudly until the laugh turned into a cough.

'Very sorry to bother you,' said Jane, edging away.

'No trouble, I'm sure,' said the woman, closing the door.

They walked quickly away.

'I think she was one of *those* women,' said Anne.

'What women?'

Anne blushed. 'You know . . . what they call women of the night.'

Jane stood still. 'You mean a *prostitute*?'

Anne nodded and blushed even more deeply.

Jane was intrigued. 'I've never met a prostitute before,' she said.

'I should hope not,' said Anne, shocked.

They drew a blank at the address in Old Compton Street. The windows were barred and it looked as though it was a shop.

'I suppose we could come back another time,' said Jane, uncertainly.

'Or you could telephone them,' said Anne. 'There's a phone box outside your flat, isn't there?'

Jane brightened. 'Yes, I suppose we could do that – or ask Mum to do it during the week.'

They walked on quickly, across to Wardour Street. The road was bigger and wider here and they didn't feel quite so conspicuous, but Jane knew that Anne was getting more anxious by the minute. She squeezed her hand.

'Don't worry,' she said. 'We'll just try the address here, then we'll head back to Montagu Square.'

Anne smiled with relief.

They found the place and stood outside looking at it. Jane felt suddenly very uneasy.

'Is it a house or an office?' said Anne.

Jane shrugged. 'Difficult to tell,' she said. 'There's nothing to say, either way. Just the number.'

'Come on, then,' said Anne. 'Let's get it over with, then we can get out of here.'

And this time it was Anne who banged hard on the front door with the brass knocker.

Jane had an inexplicable urge to run away, but the door was opened almost immediately by a well turned out, brassy-looking woman, also heavily made up.

'Yes?' she said.

'Does Peter Daniels live here?' asked Jane, finding her voice at last.

The woman gave her a hard stare. 'What do you want with Mr Daniels?' she said.

Jane couldn't explain why she felt so nervous in front of this woman. Some deep instinct told her to take care what she said and she hesitated, trying to marshal her thoughts. But Anne broke in. 'My friend's from Australia,' she said breathlessly. 'Her ancestors used to run Abigail's Gowns.'

At the mention of Abigail's Gowns, the woman's expression hardened. She said nothing.

'She's trying to trace her English family,' said Anne. 'And she thinks Mr Daniels may be a relation.'

'Hasn't she got a tongue in her head?' said the woman, looking at Jane.

'It's true,' said Jane quietly. 'I *am* trying to trace my English family.'

The woman continued to look at the girls for a moment, then she said, 'Wait here.'

She left the door open as she walked back into the house and there was the sound of voices. The woman was talking softly to a man, but the girls could hear snatches of her conversation: 'cock and bull story about Australian relations' . . . 'bit young for you'.

Jane swallowed nervously. 'I don't like this,' she whispered. 'Let's go.'

But it was too late. Just as they turned away, a man appeared in the doorway.

'I'm Peter Daniels,' he said, extending his hand. 'Come in and tell me all about these relations of mine.'

# 7

## Bedford, April, present day

*K*eith had already got some way ahead of us before we
set off, so we had to run to keep him in sight.

'What if he turns round?' I gasped. 'He'll recognize
us.'

Katie linked her arm in mine. 'If it comes to it,' she said,
'then we'll just have to face up to him.'

I suppose she was right. After all, what could he do to us
in broad daylight? But all the same, I'd rather he didn't see
us at all.

Suddenly, he slowed up and felt in his pocket.

'Someone's phoned him,' whispered Katie.

She was right. He was walking slowly, now, speaking into
his phone. We slowed up, too, keeping as far away as possible
without losing sight of him. At last, he snapped shut his
phone and put it back in his pocket. He began walking fast
again, then he looked at his watch, stopped, took his phone
out once more and made another call.

We waited, expecting him to go on walking, but he stayed

where he was, then strolled over to a shop front and leant against the wall.

We waited, too, puzzled.

'P'raps he's meeting someone,' said Katie. But some time went by and nothing happened.

'Hey,' she said suddenly, pointing to a side street a few metres away. 'If we go down this street here and double back, we'll come out on the corner, on the other side of the shop. He won't see us and we can see who he's meeting.'

I didn't want to get any closer, but Katie wouldn't listen to me. She took off and so I followed her. We ran down the narrow side street, turned left at the end, then left again.

'See,' she said, panting. 'Just down there, on the corner. That's the other side of the shop.'

'What if he walks round the corner?' I said.

'Well, if he does, we'll front up to him,' said Katie. 'We've got nothing to lose.'

I was trembling. Katie doesn't know Keith like I do.

Slowly, we walked down the street to the end and flattened ourselves against the wall. Katie inched forward and peered round the corner, then her head shot back.

'He's still there,' she whispered.

'What's he doing?'

'Just looking down the road,' she said. 'I'm sure he's arranged to meet someone here.'

My stomach was churning. Please God, I thought, don't let him see us. I just stood there, beside Katie, making myself as flat as I could while, from time to time, she peered round the corner.

She clutched my hand. 'There's a taxi coming,' she said. 'It's slowing down . . . yep, he's moving forward.'

Then, before I could stop her, she walked casually round the corner. I stayed where I was, frozen with fear.

I heard Keith's voice then. Not clearly, just a murmur. But I'd recognize it anywhere and it sent a shudder right through me. Then I heard a car draw away. I didn't move a muscle.

A few moments later, Katie skipped round the corner.

'Got it!' she shouted, punching the air with her fist.

'What?'

'An address. Where he's going!'

'How?'

Katie grinned. 'I just walked round and stared into the shop window,' she said. 'Pretended I was fascinated by all sorts of dreary business systems, or whatever it is they're selling there.'

'Didn't he see you?'

'Nope. I had my back to him and he was leaning towards the cab driver to give him the address.'

'Where is it?'

'Ah. Brace yourself, petal. This is the bad bit.'

I swallowed. 'Where?' I repeated.

Then she mentioned a number in a street.

A street that is very close to where we live.

# London, June 1947

Jane didn't want to take the outstretched hand; every instinct told her to get out of this place, but she found her hand held firmly and before she knew what was happening, she was being pulled inside. Anne followed nervously behind.

Peter Daniels looked at them and smiled but there was no warmth in the smile.

I don't trust him, thought Jane. Florrie was right. I should never have come here.

He led the way into the front-room. It was dark and gloomy and full of clutter. Large heavy chairs draped with lacy antimacassars, a dark red carpet with a floral pattern, a big sideboard made of some dark wood, ornate lamps dotted around the place and a central electric light bulb hanging from the ceiling, covered with a red lampshade.

And framed photographs everywhere. Mostly, Jane noticed, of scantily clad women.

It didn't look very homely.

Jane felt more and more uncomfortable. She shot a quick glance at Anne, who was frowning and biting her lip.

The woman who had opened the door to them had disappeared, but they could hear her speaking to someone at the end of the passage. Then the telephone rang and Jane jumped. The woman's conversation was cut short and they heard the tip-tap of high-heeled shoes walking along the passage, then the voice again as she picked up the receiver.

'Sit down, young ladies,' said Peter Daniels, showing them to a brown, over-stuffed sofa at the end of the room.

Jane and Anne sat close to each other, perching uncomfortably on the edge of the sofa.

Peter Daniels looked directly at Jane. 'So, tell me, dear. How did you come to find me?' His voice was smooth, but there was a hint of malice in it.

Jane cleared her throat. She must be careful what she said to this man. She didn't want to get anyone in trouble.

'We found out you had owned Abigail's Gowns,' she said simply. 'And my father's ancestors had started up the business about a hundred years ago I think.'

'Is that so?' said Peter Daniels. 'Isn't that interesting?'

But he didn't look at all interested. 'And how did you come to find out where I lived?' he persisted.

Anne opened her mouth to speak, but Jane jumped in. 'It was just luck,' she said firmly. 'We thought you might still live in Soho, so we looked up all the P Danielses in Soho in the telephone book.'

The man's face visibly relaxed. 'What clever young ladies you are,' he said. Then he went on, 'Yes. Abigail's. A sad business that. A pity to close something down which had lasted all that time, but there was no custom to be had.'

'Was that because of the war?' asked Anne, innocently.

'Yes, dear. No one wanted lovely dresses any more. A sad day for me when I sold it off to the insurance people, I can tell you.'

Jane thought of Florrie's words. 'Couldn't you have kept it going?' she asked. 'Making uniforms and things.'

Peter Daniels' face hardened. 'No, not at all. Wrong machines, wrong trade.' Then he changed the subject. 'So, tell me about these Australian ancestors,' he said.

Jane told him, as quickly as she could, all that Amy had told her. About Amos, who had come to Australia, about his Aunt Abbie who had started the dress-making business last century and about her daughter, Victoria, who they thought had continued the business.

There was a large grandfather clock in the corner of the room, ticking loudly. More than once, Peter Daniels' eyes slid towards it. It was obvious he was bored.

'Well, young lady,' he said, when Jane had finished. 'I don't know what I can do for you.'

Jane took her courage in both hands. 'Have you any other family, Mr Daniels? Brothers or sisters, children?'

Peter Daniels looked down at his hands. 'I don't see any of my family,' he said, and there was an edge to his voice. 'They're all country folk. I've no idea where they are.'

Jane frowned. She was sure he was lying, but what could she do?

She stood up. 'Well, thank you for seeing us,' she said.

'A pleasure, my dear. Always delighted to see pretty girls.'

Jane felt a shiver of disgust go through her.

'And where did you say you are staying?' he asked.

'With Jane's mother,' said Anne, before Jane could stop her.

Jane nudged her sharply. 'We're staying in Baker Street,' she said, mentioning the first street that came into her head.

'Baker Street, eh? What number, dear?'

'One hundred and fifteen,' said Jane, wildly plucking a number from nowhere.

'Ah, well, maybe I'll come and call on you and your mother soon. And we can talk about family matters.'

Jane nodded dumbly. She was desperate to get out of this place as soon as she could. She edged away from the sofa towards the door.

And then she saw it!

On top of the dresser, along with all the other photographs, there was one of a youngish man in uniform. Before she could stop herself, she pointed at it.

'Who's that?' she said and her voice was hoarse.

Peter Daniels looked up sharply. 'That? Oh, that's

my brother James, poor man. He was the only relation I liked, but they all poisoned him against me.'

'Where is he now?' asked Jane. And there was such desperation in her voice that Anne shot her a nervous glance.

Peter Daniels shrugged. 'Went through the war, poor man. Came back shellshocked. He's in an asylum somewhere. No idea where, though.'

His face went blank and the girls knew that he wasn't going to be any more forthcoming. He came a bit closer to them.

'Now, before you go, young ladies,' he said, 'let me make a note of that address in Baker Street again.'

He turned away briefly to get some paper and a pencil from a desk.

Quickly, Jane picked up the photo and looked on the back. She had replaced it before he turned round to them again.

'What was that house number again?'

'. . . Er . . .' Jane couldn't remember what number she had said.

'One hundred and fifteen,' said Anne loudly. Jane breathed again.

At last, they were out of the door and walking, as fast as they dared, down Wardour Street.

'He was *horrible!*' said Jane. 'Let's get away from here.'

They didn't speak again until they were a good distance from Wardour Street.

'Why did you ask about that photo?' said Anne, when they paused for breath.

Jane turned to face her. 'Because,' she said slowly, 'the man in the photo looked exactly like my father.'

'What!'

Jane nodded. 'It gave me a nasty turn, I can tell you,' she said. 'I know it can't have been him, but it *must* be a relation!'

'We can't go back there,' said Anne.

'No. I don't ever want to see that man again. I'm sure he's doing something really unpleasant – that's why I gave him a false address. But I'd like to find the man that looks so much like my father.'

'It will be like looking for a needle in a haystack,' said Anne. 'You'll never find him.'

Jane looked at her. 'We know his name – James Daniels.'

'Yes, but you heard what that horrible Peter Daniels said. His brother was shellshocked in the war and he's in an asylum. He could be anywhere.'

'*If* Peter Daniels is telling the truth,' said Jane. 'I wouldn't trust him to tell the truth, would you?'

Anne shook her head.

'And there's another thing,' continued Jane. 'The photo was taken by a studio in a place called Marlborough. I saw it on the back.'

'Marlborough!' exclaimed Anne. 'That's near where I live!'

They looked at each other. Anne suddenly smiled. 'Would you like to come and stay with me in the holidays?' she asked.

Jane squeezed Anne's hand. 'You bet I would!'

They made their way slowly back to Montagu Square. While they were still in Soho, Anne kept glancing behind her. 'You don't think he's following us, do you?' she asked.

Jane shivered. 'Oh, I hope not.' And she, too, looked back, but there was no sign of him.

Once they were over Oxford Street and turning for home, Jane suddenly stopped and turned to Anne. 'I don't think we should tell Mum about the brother,' she said slowly. 'Not until we know more ourselves.'

'Why not?'

Jane frowned. 'It's just . . . well, he looked *so* like my father. I think it would upset Mum terribly to see him, especially if he's all jerky and funny.'

Anne nodded. They both knew what 'shellshocked' could mean. 'Maybe you're right. We'll keep it to ourselves for the moment.'

It was late afternoon by the time they got back to the flat. Amy had just come in from the hospital and she looked exhausted, but she raised a smile to greet them.

'Have you had a good day? Did you find out anything?'

Jane and Anne had rehearsed what they were going to say.

'Yes, but it wasn't very nice, I'm afraid.'

They told her about finding where Abigail's Gowns had been and of Florrie's warning about Peter Daniels. And then about tracking him down.

Amy's eyes lit up, briefly. 'A real relation!' she breathed. 'How exciting!'

Jane shot Anne a look. 'He was really nasty, Mum. Honestly, you don't want to have anything to do with him.'

'He was horrible,' said Anne.

Amy looked disappointed. 'Did he say anything about other relations?' she asked hopefully.

'Only that none of them spoke to him and that he had no idea where they were,' said Jane.

Amy frowned. 'I wonder if that's really true?' she said.

'Probably not,' said Anne. 'But I don't want to see him ever again.'

Amy put her hand on Anne's shoulder. 'I'm sorry you had such an unpleasant experience, dear. I should never have let you two go off on your own like that.'

'You couldn't know we'd find him and that he'd be so nasty,' said Anne.

Jane didn't want to talk any more about Peter Daniels, so she changed the subject. 'Anne's asked me to go and stay with her in the holidays. Please may I go, Mum?'

Amy smiled at Anne. 'Why, that's very kind of you, dear. Are you sure you can manage an extra person?'

'Father would be pleased for me to have some company,' she said simply. 'It's difficult for him since Mother died.'

'Yes, it must be. I'm so sorry, Anne,' said Amy quietly. And she turned away, but not before Jane saw that her eyes were full of tears.

She still misses Dad terribly, she thought. All the more reason for keeping quiet about this relation who looked so much like him.

'I won't be gone for long,' said Jane, suddenly feeling guilty. 'And David will be here with you, won't he?'

Amy smiled. 'David seems to have all sorts of plans of his own,' she said. 'But I won't be lonely.'

It was only much later, after they had eaten and were about to leave to go back to school, that Jane asked Amy about Ernest Liddle.

Amy got up and walked over to the window which overlooked the square. Then she turned to face them. 'He died this afternoon, dear,' she said, quietly. 'It was quite peaceful.'

# 8

## Bedford, April, present day

*A*fter she'd told me, I just stood staring at Katie with my mouth open.

'You know what we're going to do, don't you?' she said, after a moment.

'What?' I whispered.

'We're going to stake out his place, then wait until he goes out and somehow break in and have a look through his stuff.'

'Break in? Don't be stupid!'

'You got a better plan?'

'Well . . . no. But, even if we did, where would that get us?'

Katie shrugged. 'We might get some real evidence against him. I dunno, something to show he's been pestering you.'

'Katie! If we broke into his place and stole something, we could hardly go to the police with it, could we? "Excuse me, officer, I just decided to break into this bloke's place on the off-chance he had some incriminating papers lying about . . ." '

112

Katie grinned. 'Look, we've outwitted him once – with the party and everything. That worked out well, didn't it?'

'Yeah. But that was different. And even then, it ended badly, with Mum in hospital.'

And suddenly, I had this image of Mum lying there, helpless, with that awful creep sitting beside her, holding her hand. I started to cry.

Katie put her arm round me. But that made me cry even more. She handed me some tissues.

'Come on,' she said. 'Keep strong. We'll work something out.'

We made our way slowly back to my house. It was a long way and I half-wished we'd ordered a taxi, too. But we were too broke and it might have been the one that had had Keith in it! The thought of sitting where he'd just been gave me the heaves.

On the way back, we made a plan. Well, Katie did all the planning and the talking. I was too stunned and upset to think straight. She's very persuasive, is Katie, and sometimes it's less effort just to go along with her and agree.

When we got home, Gran had another meal ready. Honestly, I love her to bits, but she seems to think I need feeding the whole time! But, I have to admit, I did feel better when I'd eaten.

'Katie's staying the night, Gran,' I said. 'That's okay, isn't it?'

'Of course,' said Gran, looking pleased.

'But first I'm taking Becky clubbing,' said Katie to Gran.

'It'll cheer her up and we've only got a few days of holiday left.'

Gran looked worried then. She always looks worried when I say I'm going out.

'It's okay, Gran,' I said. 'I'll have my mobile on all the time.'

'All right, dear,' she said, anxiously. But she was frowning.

'Oh, don't fuss so,' said Grandad. 'Let them go out and enjoy themselves.'

'Well, do be careful, won't you?' said Gran.

If only she knew, I thought, what we were really going to do, she'd have every reason to be anxious!

But at last, with groaning stomachs, and with Gran's warnings ringing in our ears, we managed to get away.

It was getting dark by this time, but that suited our plan.


## London, July 1947

For the final few weeks of term, Jane had been really happy. Anne's friendship had helped and now she had got to know other girls, too. And she had begun to understand about the English way of doing things, the reserve, the manners, the rules — and the good things. The sense of tradition, the ironic humour, the gradual acceptance of someone who, to these English girls, must have seemed very strange at first.

The summer term had ended now and Jane and

David and Amy had had a good ten days together getting to know London better. A lot of David's friends lived in London and were day boys at his school, so they came to visit and Amy became friendly with some of their parents. It was a happy and relaxed time.

Sometimes the twins caught Amy looking thoughtful and Jane knew that she had been hit hard by Ernest's death. He was her last link with John. The person who had been closest to him when he was dying. But she was often funny and carefree, too. This was a new and different life for her and, without all the ties and responsibilities of the Melbourne hotel and the relations back there, she could make a life for herself here.

One evening, when she was alone with the twins, she said, 'Are you happy to stay here for a while – in England, I mean?'

Jane glanced swiftly at David. He was rocking back and forth on his chair.

'I don't want to stay here for ever,' he said. 'But I don't mind staying on for a bit.'

'And what about you, Jane?'

Jane thought wistfully of the friends back in Melbourne, of the informal life they had left behind. And then of Anne and her new friends, here.

'Yes,' she said slowly. 'For a bit longer, but not for ever.'

Amy's face relaxed. 'I never meant for ever,' she said.

'Perhaps we could spend Christmas here and then go back for the start of the school year in Melbourne.'

Jane thought that Christmas seemed a long way away. But perhaps it would be fun to celebrate Christmas in winter-time for once.

'Well,' said Amy firmly, 'if we're going to be here for another few months, I must try to find a job.'

Both the twins looked up. 'Why?' asked David.

Amy smiled. 'Because the money won't last for ever, David. And, anyway, I should like to do some work.' She paused. 'It can get lonely when you are both at school.'

No more was said of it then, but Jane had a niggling worry at the back of her mind. If her mother found some sort of job, would she want to go back to Australia? She remembered how involved Amy had been in the hotel; it had been an enormous part of her life and a big wrench when she and the rest of Dad's family had made the decision to sell up.

Later that evening, while Amy was out making some telephone calls from the box on the corner, Jane spoke to David about meeting Peter Daniels. He knew that she and Anne had been to see him and that he was unpleasant, but she hadn't told him about the photo.

'Haven't you told Mum?' asked David.

Jane shook her head. 'He looked so like Father,' she said. 'And if we do find him and he is shellshocked, well . . .'

David saw the point. 'Yes,' he said slowly. 'It would be horrible for Mum to see him like that.'

'We may never find him,' said Jane. 'But it's worth a try.'

'And you're going to stay with Anne and see what you can find out?'

Jane nodded. 'I'm going down by train tomorrow,' she said.

David grinned. 'I've a good mind to come and join in the hunt,' he said.

'Oh, I don't think . . .'

David gave her a soft punch on the arm. 'Don't worry, I won't interfere with your silly girls' games!'

Jane was about to retort when the door into the flat opened. 'Don't say anything to Mum,' she whispered.

'Course not.'

'Promise?'

'Of *course* I promise, you idiot.'

Then Amy walked into the room.

The next day, Amy and David went with Jane to Paddington Station. It was huge and rather frightening, but at last they found the ticket office and were directed to the platform where the train for Marlborough stood waiting, belching out steam and soot.

As it drew out of the station, Jane waved from the window at the diminishing figures of her mother and brother. Then some gritty bits of soot flew into her face and she ducked her head inside the carriage and groped for her handkerchief to remove a smut from her streaming eye. By the time she had done this, the train had turned the corner and the platform at Paddington was out of sight.

Jane hadn't been out of London before and she was delighted when the grimy buildings were left behind and the train started winding its way through the countryside.

The trees were in full leaf, the fields full of yellow corn or of cattle. It was so unlike the great scorched, sweeping plains of the Western District of Australia where she'd sometimes been, or the bush out at Gippsland when she'd gone with William once to see where Amos and his father had started their hotel business.

By comparison, the countryside here was small and pretty and green – so green! Jane had brought a book to read on the journey, but it lay unopened in her lap as the train chugged west. At every stop, Jane stared anxiously at the signs. Anne had told her that she would have to change trains at Savernake and she didn't want to miss it. As it turned out, a lot of people got out then, so Jane followed them into another, tiny, train, with just two coaches, which wound its way up a branch line to Marlborough.

When, finally, the train ground slowly into the

station, Jane was already standing by the door, clutching her suitcase in her gloved hand.

Gingerly, she stepped down from the high train on to the platform and looked about her.

A man in a uniform and peaked cap was instantly at her side. 'Porter, Miss?' he said.

'Er. No. No thank you. I . . . I'm being met.'

'Looks like these are the people meeting you, Miss,' he said, touching his cap and pointing up the platform.

Anne was there, waving at her and running to meet her. And behind her was a tall, serious-looking man, coming forward more slowly.

Anne reached her, puffing and out of breath, and squeezed her hand.

'Jane, it's good to see you. Was the train journey all right? Was your mother all right about you coming?'

Jane nodded. The man had reached her now, too.

'Father,' said Anne, 'this is my friend Jane.'

The man put out his hand and shook Jane's outstretched hand firmly. 'Delighted to meet another Australian,' he said.

'Another?' asked Jane.

'Father fought with some Australians during the war,' explained Anne.

'Oh,' said Jane shyly.

They walked along the platform and out into the station yard.

As Anne's father was putting Jane's case into the car, Anne whispered to her. 'I've done a bit of looking about,' she said.

'What do you mean?'

'I've found out a bit about the Daniels family.'

'*What!*'

Anne nodded. 'I'll tell you when we're alone.'

So Jane had to contain her curiosity while Anne's father drove them away from the station and out into the countryside.

Jane had wondered whether they'd bring a car to meet her or whether they'd travel by bus. Petrol was still rationed and people didn't use their cars very often.

Anne's house was quite a long way from the town, but at last her father stopped the car. 'Here we are,' he said, heaving Jane's case from the back.

Jane got out and looked up at the house. 'It's lovely,' she said.

'Lovely!' said Anne, surprised. 'It's falling down and everything keeps going wrong.'

'But it's so pretty!'

Anne's father stopped and put the case down. 'It *is* pretty, isn't it?' he said, smiling. 'I hope we'll be able to stay here,' he added, so quietly that neither of the girls heard him.

It was quite a small house – and very old, according to Anne – but beautifully proportioned and standing in a large, rather overgrown garden which sloped down to a stream at the back.

'It's just like I've always imagined an English cottage in the country. All pretty and old and with lots of flowers everywhere.'

Anne and her father both laughed. Anne took her arm. 'Come inside,' she said. 'And I'll show you your room.'

Anne led the way through the hall and up a staircase with a wooden handrail which was coiled round at the bottom and gleamed with the polishing it had received from generations of hands going up and down over the years. Anne's father followed them up with the suitcase.

Anne stopped on the landing at the top. 'Here you are!' she said, flinging open the first door.

Jane stepped inside. 'It's lovely!' she said, her face breaking into a huge smile. And indeed it was.

As she looked round the room, with its well-worn rugs and faded curtains and covers, and the small window with tiny leaded panes which overlooked the garden, she felt instantly at home.

Anne's father put down her case. 'Well, I'll leave you two to gossip,' he said. 'Then bring Jane down to meet Mrs Walker when you're ready, Anne.'

He walked out and closed the door behind him.

'Who's Mrs Walker?' asked Jane.

'The housekeeper,' said Anne, making a face. Then

she grinned. 'She's all right, I suppose. Just a bit old-fashioned.'

Jane sat on the bed and stretched her hands above her head.

'Oh, it's so good to be out of the town,' she said. 'It's so quiet here.'

'Hmm. A bit too quiet,' said Anne. 'There's not much to do.'

'But you've been busy finding out about the Daniels family. Come on, tell me everything!'

Anne sat down beside her.

'I looked in the local phone book and there were several Danielses listed, but I didn't dare ring them up.'

'I don't blame you,' said Jane.

'Then, last night, I decided to ask Father if he knew any round here. His family have lived in this area for years. If anyone knows, he would.'

'And?'

'Well, of course he wanted to know *why* I was suddenly so interested, so I told him. I said you and your mother wanted to trace your father's English ancestors and there was a family called Daniels who had lived round here.'

'You didn't say anything about our visit to Peter Daniels, did you?'

Anne shook her head. 'He would have had a fit if he thought we'd been wandering round Soho!'

Jane grinned. 'So, what did he say about the Daniels family? Does he know any of them?'

Anne dug in her pocket and drew out a crumpled piece of paper.

'There a butcher called Daniels, in Marlborough, and a saddler, too. Father says they're brothers.'

'A saddler,' said Jane. 'That sounds hopeful.'

'Why?'

'Well, you remember I told you that Dad's ancestors ran a harness-making business in London,' said Jane.

'Oh yes. Of course!'

'Do you think we could go and visit these people?'

Anne nodded. 'Father says he'll help us. He could make contact with them, so they don't think it's just us trying to find out.'

Jane squeezed Anne's hand. 'That's wonderful. When can we start?'

'We can speak to Father about it,' said Anne. 'But now you'd better come and meet Mrs Walker.'

They went downstairs to the kitchen. Anne knocked on the door. 'Mrs Walker! Can we come in?'

'Why do you have to *knock*?' asked Jane, in amazement.

'It's her territory,' whispered Anne.

And before she could say more, the door was opened.

Mrs Walker looked cross. She was stout and she wore a large white apron, under which was a blouse, buttoned severely at the neck. In one hand she held a rolling pin and she was frowning.

'This your friend from London then, Miss Anne?' she said, without preamble.

'Yes, Mrs Walker, this is my friend Jane.'

Mrs Walker wiped her free hand down her apron and stuck it out towards Jane.

'Pleased to meet you, I'm sure,' she said.

Jane took the large, meaty hand and endured a hearty pumping up and down. 'It's good to meet you, too, Mrs Walker,' she said nervously.

Mrs Walker turned to Anne. 'She speaks a bit funny,' she said.

Jane smiled. She was used to the reaction by now. 'I'm from Australia, Mrs Walker,' she said.

'Oh well, that explains it then!' said Mrs Walker, who had never been further than Marlborough and had no idea where Australia was.

There was an awkward silence.

'She's trying to trace her English ancestors,' said Anne.

'Oh yes,' said Mrs Walker, turning away.

Anne looked at Jane. 'They were called Daniels,' she said loudly.

Mrs Walker stopped in her tracks and turned back to look at Jane. 'Daniels?' she said.

'Yes,' said Jane. 'Do you know anyone of that name? I think they came from round here.'

'Huh,' said Mrs Walker. 'Yes, I know some of the Daniels family.'

'What, the butcher and the saddler?' asked Anne.

'Oh yes, I know *them*,' said Mrs Walker.

'And are there any other members of the family?' asked Jane.

Mrs Walker met her eyes. 'I wouldn't go sniffing around, girl, not if I were you.'

'Why? Why not?' asked Anne.

'Because,' said Mrs Walker, attacking some pastry with the rolling pin.

'Why?' persisted Anne.

'Because there's a deal you don't know about that family, Miss Anne. And it don't do no good digging up the past.'

Jane opened her mouth to ask more, but Mrs Walker pointed her rolling pin at her.

'Now, off you go, both of you, out of my kitchen, or you won't have nothing to eat for your supper.'

### Bedford, April, present day.

*I'm writing this in the early hours. I can't believe that Katie and I have just done what we have. I'm really scared now because I think Keith may find out and, if he does, God knows what will happen.*

*We left my house just as it was getting dark. The address*

that Katie had overheard Keith giving to the cab driver was only a few streets away and we walked there in silence. Katie had pretended, all along, that she wasn't scared, but I know she was. That walk to his house seemed to take forever, even though it was so close, and I'm sure Katie was feeling just as terrified as me.

When we got to it, there was nothing different about the house. It was just a small, terraced house in a row of similar houses. He didn't own it, I was sure of that. What had he done? Had he rented it for a few months or what?

'It's so ordinary,' I said, stupidly.

'What did you expect?' hissed Katie. 'A big banner out the front saying, "Nutter lives here. Beware!"?'

We both giggled nervously then and it broke the tension.

'Come on, let's look round,' said Katie.

There were lights on in the house, so someone was in.

'For God's sake be careful,' I whispered.

I expect Katie gave me a withering look, but it was difficult to see in the dark!

There was no sign of anyone around the place. No one else walking down the street. No one going in and out of other houses. It was really quiet and spooky.

We crept round to the back of the house, but there was a high fence.

'We can't climb that!' I said.

'There's a gate in the fence, you plonker!' said Katie.

She was right. There was. And it wasn't even padlocked. Very quietly, Katie raised the latch and we crept into the back garden.

'What do we do now?' I asked.

'We watch – and wait.'

Nothing happened for ages and I was getting stiff from crouching behind a bush at the back of the garden.

Then suddenly there was some movement at the back of the house. A light snapped on and, for a moment, a figure was silhouetted against the window, drawing the curtains.

My stomach lurched. It was Keith all right.

'Do you think he's going to go to bed? Going to have an early night?' said Katie.

I shook my head. 'Not unless he's changed his habits,' I said. 'He usually went to the pub every night when he was living with us.'

'How long for?'

I shrugged. 'For about an hour. Until closing time, I guess.'

'P'raps that's what he's going to do now.'

The light at the back of the house was turned off. And a few minutes later we heard the front door slam.

We waited for a bit longer.

'We'd better check out the front,' said Katie. 'Make sure he's gone.'

We got round to the front just in time to see him walking away down the street. The house was in darkness.

'Right,' said Katie.

I felt really sick. 'Katie, please! We can't do this!'

'Think of your mum, Becky. We're doing this for her.'

I nodded silently, and miserably trailed behind Katie as she led the way back in through the fence.

'There's a window on the ground floor,' she said, snapping on her torch. 'Let's see if it's open.'

Keith was paranoid about burglar alarms and window catches and things like that. I was sure that everything would be impenetrable. Secretly, I hoped it was.

There was a sort of lean-to beside the window, full of logs. Before I could stop her, Katie had climbed on top of it and was examining the window. It was an old window, with a fanlight at the top, which was slightly open.

Katie put her hand through this and leant her body down until her hand reached the main catch. She pressed down on it and it opened.

'Bingo!' she said. 'Come on.'

We eased our bodies through the window. We didn't even have to jump. There was a radiator just below it and we balanced on that and then stepped on to a handy chair.

'Made it easy for burglars, hasn't he?' whispered Katie, grinning.

I couldn't believe it! This wasn't the security-conscious Keith I remembered. But perhaps, if he was just renting the place, he didn't care so much. But he'd still have his stuff in the house; I couldn't understand it.

Inside, we crept from room to room, only using the torch sparingly. We were very careful not to disturb things.

In the front-room downstairs was a computer and a whole lot of papers strewn over a table.

'He must use this as his office,' said Katie, shining the torch on various letters.

I was desperate to get out of the place, but I made myself think clearly.

'Is there an address of the loan company?' I asked.

Katie scanned some of the letters. 'Yep. I think this is it.'

Quickly, I brought out the pad and pencil from the pocket of my jacket. I noted down the name and address and also the names of the directors, while Katie kept looking at the other correspondence.

'It all seems pretty legit,' she said. 'Just business stuff. No threats or anything that I can see. Shall I keep looking?'

'Don't disturb anything,' I said. 'We really really don't want him to know we've been here.'

I stared at the blank screen of the computer. Suddenly I had an idea.

'Katie,' I whispered. 'Can you find his email address on any of that stuff? Not the company email – I've got that. His private email address?'

The torch flickered to and fro. 'Yep, here it is,' she said.

We wrote it down. 'Now, let's get out of here!'

'But we haven't found . . .'

'I think we've got all we need,' I said. 'I've had an idea.'

Katie took a bit of persuading, but, thank goodness, I managed to get her to leave when we did, the way we came, closing the downstairs window behind us.

Just as we had jumped down from the lean-to on to the grass below, we heard the front door slam.

My heart leapt with fright.

'My God,' I said. 'He didn't go to the pub after all. He's

only been gone ten minutes! If we'd been any longer, he would have caught us!'

Katie clutched my arm. 'Shh! Get down,' she whispered.

For a long time, we huddled together beside the lean-to, not daring to move. The light went on again in the bedroom and we waited ages until, at last, it went out and the garden was plunged into velvety darkness again. As quietly as we could, we tiptoed out through the back gate and round to the road, then, keeping close to the edge, in the darkest part of the pavement, we walked very slowly and quietly to the end of the street. But once there, we ran like hares, back to my house.

When we got back, Gran and Grandad were asleep and the house was in darkness. We went into my room and I went straight over to my computer and switched it on.

'What are you doing?' asked Katie.

'It probably won't work,' I said. 'But it's worth a try.'

'What?'

'Well, we've got his email address, so we know who his ISP is. I'm going to go on-line and see if I can tap into his emails.'

Katie frowned. 'But you don't have his password.'

'I know. But when he lived with us he used Mum's name in it. I remember him telling her once.'

'Surely he'll have changed it?'

'I don't know. If he's still so obsessed with her, perhaps it's still the same.'

The ISP's website came up on the screen and I typed in his email address. Then I tried a password.

I put Mum's name first. Then the beginning of our surname, Ford. The password had to have eight digits: 'SARAHFOR.'

'Bad login' came up on the computer.

I thought a bit. I'd have to be careful. I think you only have three goes at it and then it crashes – for security, I suppose – and you can't get in again.

I paused and closed my eyes. How would Keith think? What does he most want from Mum? In his fantasies, does he think of her in his arms? Kissing her, perhaps? I gave an involuntary shudder. Probably it would be something like that, wouldn't it? He's still desperate for her. He still wants her.

Slowly, I tapped in again. This time I put 'SFORDXXX'.

But it was no good. Again, 'bad login' came up on the screen.

'You're not going to get it, Becky,' said Katie. 'It could be anything. Any combination.'

'I bet he's put a kiss somewhere in his password,' I said grimly. 'I'll give it one last try.'

My fingers felt heavy and sticky with perspiration. If it didn't work this time, I'd blown it.

Carefully, I tried again: 'SARAHXXX'.

To my amazement, the computer whirred into action.

'My God! You've done it!' shouted Katie, who was looking over my shoulder.

I punched the air with my fist. 'Yeah!' I shouted. 'Got you!'

We stared at the screen.

131

'There's so much on it!' said Katie. 'Masses and masses of stuff.'

I opened up various emails he'd received and sent. And some that he'd trashed but were still in the 'deleted' box. I couldn't believe what I was seeing.

The words started to swim before my eyes. I felt sick.

Katie put her hands on my shoulders. 'Don't read any more now,' she said quietly. 'We'll go through it all in the morning.'

I turned back and looked at her. 'He is seriously sick,' I whispered. 'I never guessed . . .'

Then I put my head in my hands and started to cry.

Katie closed down the computer. 'Come on,' she said gently. 'It's late. Let's get some sleep and talk about it in the morning.'

'We need to print some of that stuff out, before he gets rid of it.'

'There'll be plenty more,' said Katie, grimly. 'Come on. Get to bed. You're knackered.'

We went to bed then, but I couldn't sleep. That's why I'm writing this now, at two o'clock in the morning, sitting on the edge of my bed. I'm not cold but I'm shivering so much that I can hardly hold the pen.

To think that Mum once thought she was going to marry that man.

It's so much worse than I thought. We're going to have to act quickly. But we're going to have to be very very careful.

I wish Matt was here. I've just send him a text: 'Phone me. Urgent.'

# 9

## Marlborough, July 1947

They had a pleasant supper that evening. Mrs Walker had gone home, but she had left a meal ready for them. Anne's father was kind if a bit awkward, but Jane could see how difficult it must be for him, trying to work and to look after Anne and the cottage. And it must be lonely for Anne, too, sometimes. She said that she had some good friends nearby, but no one within walking distance, and transport was difficult.

'Now, about these relations of yours,' said Anne's father, after they had eaten.

'Well, I don't *know* if they are relations,' said Jane, 'but I do know that my father had ancestors called Daniels that probably lived round here.'

She thought again of the photo in Peter Daniels' house. It was a weak clue – not much to go on. Mentally, she shrugged, telling herself it really didn't matter if they weren't her relations. It would be an adventure, anyway. And she was intrigued by Mrs

Walker's reaction when they'd mentioned the name Daniels. Maybe she knew about Peter Daniels, too.

Anne's father stood up from the table. 'I'll telephone them now,' he said. 'And explain why you want to see them.'

He scraped his chair back and walked into the hall outside, where the telephone stood on a table.

'We've only just had the telephone put in,' said Anne. 'But Father doesn't like me to use it much because of the expense.'

The girls cleared the table and carried the dishes through into the kitchen.

Jane dumped the dirty plates in the sink and started to wash up, but Anne stopped her, saying that Mrs Walker would do them in the morning.

'It won't take a minute,' said Jane.

'No. Really. Mrs Walker doesn't like it.'

Jane thought Mrs Walker should be pleased, but she didn't say so and instead asked Anne, 'What does your father do? What's his work?'

Anne frowned. 'It's a family business and it's based in Swindon,' she said. 'They make stringed instruments – violins, violas, cellos.'

'But you aren't musical, are you?' said Jane. 'I've never heard you play anything.'

'Oh, I can play the piano a bit, but I'm the dunce of the family. Father plays brilliantly – on any instrument. Piano, strings, brass. He's amazing.'

Jane had noticed a small grand piano in the drawing-room of the cottage. It dominated the room.

'But the trouble is, no one is buying new instruments now. I think Father's really worried about the business.'

'Because of the war?'

Anne nodded. 'The place pretty well closed down during the war because a lot of the workers signed on to fight. They'd hoped things would pick up by now, but they haven't – at least not yet – and Father doesn't know how long they can go on like this.'

'The war. The horrible war,' muttered Jane, to herself.

The war had taken her father and, with him, their business. It had taken Anne's mother and was ruining *her* father's business, too.

But they weren't unique. So many families had been affected, so many businesses ruined. And here in England, they'd been much more affected than in Australia. There'd been bombs all over the country, not just in London. Other towns had suffered terrible damage and, even here, just outside a small market town, there were bomb craters in the fields. Anne had pointed them out on the way from the station.

Anne's father came back from the phone.

'I've spoken to both families and they're happy to see you,' he said, smiling at Jane.

'Oh, thank you, that's wonderful,' said Jane, clapping her hands together. 'Can we go tomorrow?'

'Well, yes, I suppose so. They said to call in at any time.'

'But, Father . . .' began Anne.

'Yes, dear, I know what you're going to say: there's no bus tomorrow. So why don't you take the pony and trap?'

'You've got a *pony*!' exclaimed Jane.

Anne looked doubtful. 'He's fat and lazy and it takes ages to get anywhere. And there's nowhere to tie him up once we get to town.'

Anne's father smiled. 'Oh, he's not such a bad old chap.' He turned to Jane. 'I use him whenever I can, to save on petrol. Anyway,' he went on, 'there's a bus the next day if you'd rather not use him.'

Jane looked at Anne. 'Oh, please let's go in the pony and trap. It'll be fun.'

Anne sighed. 'All right, then, but don't blame me if we're slow.'

That night, lying in bed, Jane thought sleepily of what might happen the next day. Would she find out more about that man who looked so eerily like her poor dead father? Would she be able to tell Amy more about the elusive ancestors?

She turned over in bed and breathed in deeply. Around her were the night sounds and smells of the country. The occasional shriek of an owl or bark of a dog and the heady scent of the honeysuckle which clung to the wall outside her bedroom window.

And, below, coming up from the drawing-room, the sound of the piano. Jane was no musician, but even she could appreciate the skill with which Anne's father played. She half-recognized the piece; she must have heard it somewhere.

As she drifted off to sleep, the music mingled with the face of her father, staring out at her from that photo frame in the sinister house in Soho.

The next day, Jane woke late. As she came sleepily downstairs, she met Mrs Walker at the bottom, muttering darkly. 'Your breakfast's in the dining-room,' she said. 'Dried up by now, I shouldn't wonder,' she added.

'Sorry. No one woke me,' said Jane.

'Huh,' replied Mrs Walker, and stomped off to the kitchen.

Anne was in the dining-room and it was obvious she'd finished eating some time ago.

'Sorry I'm late. Mrs Walker looked cross. You should have woken me.'

Anne smiled. 'Oh don't mind Mrs Walker,' she said. 'She's just a creature of habit.'

Jane sat down and tucked into a large plate of bacon and eggs which had been kept warm on the hot plate on the sideboard. It was delicious and not dried up at all.

'Has your father left for work?' she asked, with her mouth full.

Anne nodded. 'Yes, he always leaves early. Though, with no orders coming in, I don't know what he finds to do there.'

After breakfast, Anne found Jane a pair of wellington boots to wear and they walked along the road to a nearby field. Jane stood at the gate while Anne caught the pony and led him back. He was a small, solidly built chestnut cob and his coat shone in the morning sun.

'He's lovely. What's he called?'

'Brandy.'

Jane stroked his nose.

'Can you hold him for a minute?' said Anne, passing Jane the rope. 'I've got to get all the tack out of the shed.'

There was a big shelter in the field, and part of it was a tack shed. Behind the shed was a pony trap, resting on its shafts. Anne came back with grooming things and an armful of harness. She showed Jane how to pick out the pony's hooves and how to use the brush and curry comb, then she put on the harness.

'Goodness,' said Jane. 'You are an expert at this. I wouldn't know where to begin!'

Anne smiled. 'I've ridden all my life,' she said. 'My mother was very keen and she taught me. And she taught me how to harness a pony to the trap and to drive it, too.'

Jane watched in awe as Brandy was tacked up and then backed into the shafts of the trap. Before long, everything was in place.

'All ready,' said Anne. 'Jump up.'

Jane scrambled up into the trap beside Anne, who clicked her tongue and shook the long reins gently across the pony's back.

They turned out of the field and soon Brandy was trotting along the road towards Marlborough.

It was a lovely day and Jane looked about as they drove. The corn was just turning golden, dotted with red poppies, and the grass verges were full of white and purple wild flowers.

'It's all so pretty,' she said. 'You must miss it when you're in London.'

'It's not so good in the winter,' said Anne. 'Last winter was terrible − one of the worst in living memory. We were cut off from the main road for days and days.'

'Didn't you run out of food?'

Brandy had slowed down and was eyeing the grass on the verges, so Anne flicked the reins again. 'You have to be prepared down in the country,' she said. 'We had plenty of flour to make bread, and corn for the chickens. But the snowdrifts were huge. Right up to the windows of the house. We couldn't have gone on much longer.'

Jane had never seen snow. She couldn't imagine it.

She smiled to herself. Maybe she would. Maybe they'd have a white Christmas!

At last they reached the main street in Marlborough. It wasn't a big town and there wasn't much traffic, but, as Anne had said, there was nowhere to tie up the pony, so one of them would have to stay with him.

'You go and do the asking,' said Anne. 'The butcher's over there. And the saddler's right at the other end of town, so I'll take you there when you've finished at the butcher's.'

Jane scrambled down from the trap. She patted Brandy's neck absently and then started to walk slowly towards the butcher's shop. She didn't really know what she would say when she got there, so she took her time and tried to collect her thoughts as she approached the shop. There was a long queue of women snaking out of the shop and on to the pavement. Most of them wore headscarves and carried baskets. The queue was moving slowly, but the women seemed good-tempered and resigned to waiting. Meat was still rationed and housewives had got used to waiting for what little there was. There were still many wartime restrictions in place, even now, two years after the war had ended.

Jane wondered whether she should join the queue and wait her turn, but what would she say when she got to the counter? 'I don't want any meat but are you my father's relation?' She smiled to herself. No, she couldn't do that.

She passed the end of the queue, went down an alley beside the butcher's shop, and found the back entrance.

She hesitated for a while, then she took a deep breath, cleared her throat and knocked firmly on the door.

At first there was no answer, so she knocked again and the door was finally opened by a large woman wearing a white coat.

'Sorry, my dear,' she said, wiping her hands down the sides of her coat. 'I was helping out in the shop. What can I do for you?'

Jane explained who she was and, for a moment, the woman looked startled, but then she recovered herself.

'Oh yes. Of course. The telephone call last night. I remember.' She put out her hand. 'I'm Mrs Daniels. How do you do.'

Jane took the outstretched hand. 'If you're busy, I'll come back later,' she said, thinking of the long queue of customers.

The woman smiled. 'It's always busy,' she said. 'And there's never enough meat to go round, so we can't please everyone. Anyway, I could do with a sit down and a cuppa.'

She ushered Jane into the kitchen and put the kettle on the range. While she was waiting for the water to boil, she asked Jane where she came from and what she'd been doing in England.

'Fancy you coming all the way from Australia,' said Mrs Daniels, pouring the water into a teapot.

Jane found her easy to talk to, so she told her about school and about her mother's determination to track down her father's ancestors, and about meeting Ernest Liddle and how he'd just died.

'Oh the war,' said Mrs Daniels. 'It's hurt us all, one way and another.' She sighed. 'But we just have to get on with life, that's all we can do.' She gestured for Jane to sit down at the kitchen table, and poured her a cup of tea.

'So, dear, why is it that you think my husband's family may be something to do with your father?'

Jane explained about Abigail's Gowns, how they'd traced the dressmaking business back to Abbie, who was Amos's aunt, and then, watching Mrs Daniels closely, she said, 'I tracked down the last owner – Peter Daniels. A friend and I went to visit him in Soho.'

Jane was quite unprepared for the reaction to this. Mrs Daniels spluttered over a mouthful of tea and replaced her cup, with a clatter, into the saucer, slurping the liquid over the surface of the table.

'You did *what!*'

'I . . . we went to visit Peter Daniels.'

Mrs Daniels had gone very pale. 'You shouldn't have done that, dear. You really shouldn't.'

'I didn't like him much,' said Jane quietly.

Mrs Daniels put her hand over Jane's. 'He's an evil man, my dear. And he's ruined a lot of lives.' She passed her hand over her brow. 'I only know what my husband has told me,' she continued. 'Peter Daniels is his first cousin, but they never speak. There's no contact between them, but there's a lot of bad feeling there, I can tell you that.'

Jane nodded. She couldn't believe that this friendly woman and her husband would have anything to do with Peter Daniels. She swallowed nervously. She didn't want to push her luck, but she must find out about the man in the photo.

'When I was in Peter Daniels' house . . .' she began.

Mrs Daniels looked shocked. 'You went inside?! You were lucky you ever came out!'

Jane looked puzzled. 'What do you mean?'

But Mrs Daniels went quiet suddenly. 'I've said enough,' she said.

There was an awkward silence, then Jane continued. 'Anyway, when I was there I saw this photo of a man in uniform. It was on a sideboard.'

Mrs Daniels took a sharp breath and her hand flew to her mouth, but she didn't say anything. Jane carried on.

'He – the man in the photo – looked exactly like my father, so I was sure we must be related. Then I looked on the back of the photo and I saw it had been

143

taken in a studio here in Marlborough. That's why I came here,' she finished lamely.

'He has a photo of him in his house! How dare he!' muttered Mrs Daniels.

'Who *is* the man in the photo?' asked Jane. 'Peter Daniels said he was his brother and that he was shellshocked after the war and had been put in an institution.'

Mrs Daniels had been tracing a pattern on the wooden table with her finger. Now she raised her head and looked straight at Jane.

'Yes, dear, that's right. He is Peter Daniels' brother. He is called James and he lived near here. He was a fine man, was James, and he never said anything bad about Peter, but Peter swindled him out of his rightful inheritance, sold the business and went into something that could earn him a lot more.'

'Is he doing something illegal?'

Mrs Daniels nodded. 'And James tried to stop him. Tried to reason with him.'

'And then he went off to the war and got shellshocked?'

Mrs Daniels shook her head. 'He went off to war all right. And every time he was back on leave, he'd go and see Peter, try to get him to stop what he was doing.'

'Then what happened?'

Mrs Daniels walked across to the sink and got a

144

dish–cloth to wipe up the spilt tea. Slowly, she cleared up the puddle and then she straightened.

'Well, it wasn't shellshock, my dear, that's for sure. It was a bullet. They found James one night, lying in a Soho street, shot through the head.'

Jane looked up. 'How terrible! Was he dead?'

Mrs Daniels shook her head. 'He was left for dead, but he survived. Though, God knows, it would have been better if he had died.'

'So, where is he now?'

'He's in an institution, poor man. And he'll never come out. He can't speak or see and half his brain's been blown away.'

'I'm so sorry,' said Jane, quietly, thinking of that photo of the man so like her own father and being thankful that he hadn't had to suffer this half-life.

Mrs Daniels went to the sink and squeezed out the dish-cloth. Still with her back to Jane, she said, 'So now you see why you must keep away from Peter Daniels.'

'Don't worry,' said Jane. 'I mean to.'

Mrs Daniels looked at her watch.

'If you'll excuse me, dear, I'd better get back to the shop now. If you're going to see my husband's brother, the saddler, he'll be able to help you more about family history. He's got an interest in such things.'

Jane stood up. 'Yes, I'm sorry I've taken up so much of your time.'

'It's been a pleasure to meet you, dear. Come and

see us any time, and bring your mother, too. But, better not mention Peter Daniels or James to my husband or to his brother when you see him. It doesn't do to start stirring things up.'

Jane walked towards the door. 'Can you tell me what Peter Daniels is involved in?'

Mrs Daniels suddenly looked stern. 'It's not for the ears of a young girl like yourself,' she said primly.

'Is it something to do with prostitution?'

Mrs Daniels went very red. 'You shouldn't know about such things!' she said, looking shocked.

But Jane had her answer.

They said goodbye and Jane promised to call again. Just as she was going out of the door, she turned back. 'You think that Peter Daniels tried to murder his own brother, don't you?'

Mrs Daniels nodded silently. Then she said, 'But it's all in the past now, dear. Please don't stir things up again by talking of him.'

'I won't,' said Jane. 'I promise.'

Thoughtfully, she walked back down the high street and joined Anne, who was standing beside Brandy's head, talking to him. She looked up when Jane approached.

'You've been gone ages,' she said. 'Any luck?'

Jane nodded. 'Yes. I've found out a lot. I'll tell you everything later.'

'D'you still want to go to the saddler's?'

146

'Yes, if you don't mind.'

Jane was quiet as Anne turned Brandy's head back into the traffic and he trotted down the road to the other end of town. There was a lot to think about and she hoped she wasn't getting into something she couldn't handle. What if Peter Daniels had followed them that day they visited him? Or had them followed? She shivered, despite the warmth of the day.

Mr Daniels, the saddler, was more than happy to talk about family history and Jane spent a long time with him as he stitched and hammered, occasionally peering over his half-glasses at her.

He knew all about Abigail's Gowns, and told her that it had been passed down from Abbie to her daughter Victoria and so on, down the family, to Victoria's children and their children's children.

'The family is all descended from James and Victoria, who were Abbie's children, or from Jim, who was Abbie's brother, and his grandson. Then they all had children and so on. Me and my brother are directly descended from Victoria.

'You know,' he said, 'at the outbreak of war, a lot of the family still lived in London, close to each other, in the same street, but during the war nearly all their houses were destroyed in the Blitz. It was terrible.'

'Did you lose a lot of relations then?'

Mr Daniels paused. 'Yes,' he said quietly. 'But then so did many other families.' He picked up another sheet of leather to trim. 'Once Abigail's Gowns was sold, the family all split up. They live all over the place now.'

Jane watched him closely. He certainly wasn't going to mention Peter Daniels, so neither would she.

Jane wrote down some of the names of the direct descendants of Abbie's, to give to Amy, and a brief idea of where they lived, and she promised that she'd bring her mother to visit some time soon.

At last, they were driving back to Anne's house.

'I've found out so much for Mum,' said Jane. 'I'm really grateful to you for waiting all that time.'

'I didn't mind,' said Anne. 'But I think we'll go swimming in the river this afternoon instead of chasing any more relations.'

'I'd like that,' said Jane.

Anne shot her a glance. 'Are you going to tell me all the dark family secrets, then?'

Jane smiled 'Not now. I'll tell you later, though, I promise.'

A week later, Jane left to go back to London, promising to return, with her mother, before the end of the holidays so that Amy could meet these new relations.

Amy and David were at Paddington to meet her and, all the way back to Montagu Square in the cab, Jane chatted about the nice butcher and saddler and their families and how they must all go and visit them.

Amy was astonished. 'My goodness, Jane. You've been busy. How on earth did you find out so much? And how did you know these relations lived in Marlborough?'

Jane reddened. 'Oh, the man in Soho told me,' she said, but she changed the subject quickly and started asking David what he'd been doing.

David described his activities in detail – he'd been watching the tennis at Wimbledon, going to cricket matches, visiting friends.

After a while, Jane's eyes glazed with boredom and she stopped listening. By the time they turned off Baker Street towards Montagu Square, her thoughts were elsewhere as she stared vacantly out of the window.

Then suddenly she was wide awake. There, in the street, was a figure she recognized. A figure she was never likely to forget. Standing on the corner, talking earnestly to another man, was Peter Daniels.

As the cab reached the flat and they all got out, Jane looked back.

He was still there – and he was looking in their direction.

# 10

## Bedford, April, present day

*I must have fallen asleep eventually, because I was woken early by the ring of my mobile phone, which was lying on the table beside my bed. I snatched it up and saw Matt's name come up on the screen.*

*Typical Matt, he came straight to the point. 'What's up, Becky?'*

*It was so good to hear his voice.*

*'It's Keith,' I said simply. And I could almost hear him bristling on the other end.*

*'Go on,' he said.*

*'I managed to access his emails last night.'*

*'What! How?'*

*'Never mind how. I got lucky.' I paused. 'Anyway, Matt, listen carefully. There's a lot of really dodgy, sick stuff on there – pornography, people who get their kicks from violence, that sort of stuff. I've not had time to look at it all, but I think there may be enough to nail him.'*

*Matt was silent for so long that I thought he'd gone.*

'Matt?'

'I'm still here, Becky. Just trying to take this in. The bastard!'

'What shall we do, Matt? This may be our only chance and I don't want to mess up. I'm really scared.'

'Print out as much as you can – so you've got evidence before it's wiped.'

'Yes, we were going to do that this morning. But it makes me sick to my stomach just looking at some of this.'

'Think of Mum. Do it for her.'

I felt a lump come to my throat. 'Okay,' I said huskily. 'Then what?'

'Then I think you should get on to Mum's lawyer friend, Susan Bradfield. Get on to her right away. Go and see her. Show her the stuff. She'll know whether you've got enough to go back to the police.'

'Okay,' I said again. 'But she'll want to know how I got hold of it.'

'How did you?'

'Katie and I broke into the place where he's living and got his private email address.'

Matt laughed. 'Better not tell anyone about that,' he said. 'Just say you remembered the address from when he lived with us – and the password, too, I suppose.'

'Well, it's partly true,' I said.

There were voices in the background.

'Becky, I've got to go now, but keep me up to date. I'll try to come down to see Mum at the weekend.'

I disconnected and sat holding the phone for a moment. I

felt exhausted and frightened. But Matt and Katie were there for me. Somehow, if I was very careful, we might be able to bring an end to this nightmare at last.

I got dressed and woke Katie. We started printing out all the filth, trying not to look at it too closely, though we had to go for the worst stuff to make an impression.

It was vile.

Of course, Gran had cooked us a huge breakfast, but I couldn't eat a thing, I felt so churned up inside. Gran looked worried. She said I looked pale. So I said I just had a terrible hangover. She looked disapproving then, but at least it shut her up!

Then, at nine, I rang Susan Bradfield from my mobile and made an appointment to see her that afternoon. At first she didn't want to see me without Gran or Grandad there, but in the end I persuaded her.

Then Katie and I went to the hospital. I badly wanted to see Mum.

'What if Keith's visiting?' said Katie.

'When did he come yesterday?'

Katie frowned. 'Around lunch-time wasn't it?'

'Well, let's hope he keeps to a routine.'

As we went up in the lift to the ward, we kept looking round, but there was no sign of Keith.

While we were walking down the corridor, someone dropped something and we both jumped and spun round, clutching at each other instinctively.

The ward sister recognized me and came up. She was

smiling. 'Your mum opened her eyes last night,' she said. 'And she's looking around.'

I wanted to cry but I swallowed hard and managed a whisper. 'Does that mean she's getting better?'

The sister nodded. 'Well, it means that she's no longer unconscious,' she said cautiously. 'But of course there's no way of telling how much improvement she will make.'

When we reached Mum's bed, her eyes were open and she was staring ahead.

I sat down beside her and held her hand.

'Mum.'

And then she turned her head and looked at me. Really looked at me.

And smiled.

I started to cry then. I couldn't stop myself.

She squeezed my hand and I could see that she was trying to say something. I put my ear near to her mouth.

'Don't cry, darling,' she whispered.

But of course that really set me off. I turned to Katie, sobbing. 'She spoke! She spoke to me!'

She managed a few more words and phrases that morning, but then she started getting tired so we crept away and left her to sleep.

On the way out, I told the ward sister what had happened and she nodded.

'It's too early to say whether she'll make a full recovery, Becky, but she's certainly getting better, there's no doubt of *that. Just keep coming in to see her, as often as you can, even if it's only for a short time.'*

I wanted to tell her to stop Keith visiting, and I was just about to mention it when I stopped myself. Perhaps it would be better not to raise his suspicions.

As far as I know, he doesn't know that we know he's been visiting her.

We don't want to scare him off. Not now. Not when we're so close.

Oh God. I hope the police haven't found out where he lives and been round to see him. That would put him on his guard and he's quite capable of vanishing.

### London, August 1947

Jane tossed and turned that night in bed. Had Peter Daniels seen her? Was it just coincidence that he'd been so near their flat?

She couldn't believe it was coincidence.

The next day, she wouldn't go out alone. Amy asked her to do a simple errand and she insisted that David came too. And all the time they were away from the flat, she kept turning round and looking behind her.

'What's the matter, Jane?' asked David, more than once. 'You're acting like a startled rabbit.'

He got so exasperated with her that, in the end, she had to tell him all about Peter Daniels and their visit to his house – properly, this time, with nothing left out. And she told him what he'd done to his brother and how his cousins in Marlborough wouldn't speak of him.

David always pretended to be the worldly one, but he was obviously shocked.

'You don't think he's trying to kidnap you, do you?'

Jane almost smiled; it sounded so far-fetched. But she was too scared to smile.

'I don't think so,' she said, slowly. 'I mean . . . it would be pretty stupid, wouldn't it? I mean, Mum knows I visited him and she knows he lives in Soho.'

'I don't know,' said David. 'If he's a real criminal, then maybe you're just another young girl he can make disappear and force into a life of . . .'

'All right, all right!' said Jane, covering her ears. 'I don't want to hear any more.'

But David was getting into his stride. 'And I bet, if he's such a shady character, he wouldn't take you back to his place, anyway. If he managed to kidnap you; he must have lots of places for hiding young women.'

'David! Stop it, will you! You're making me really frightened now.'

'Don't you see, Jane? He could deny ever meeting you. I bet he's done that enough times. I expect he reckons that if you're allowed to wander around Soho on your own, you'll wander around here on your own. Easy for him to pick you up – or one of his henchmen.'

'But Anne was with me. She could tell the police about him . . .'

'He'd deny ever setting eyes on her.'

'But his wife saw us!'

'Huh!' said David, trying to sound sophisticated. 'Bet she wasn't his wife, and anyway, I expect she'd say what she was told to say.'

Jane stuck very close to David as they made their way across to Baker Street and to the greengrocer where Amy had asked Jane to buy vegetables. Her hand shook as she handed over the money and took the potatoes and spinach, and she kept glancing from side to side. David took the parcels from her.

'You know, you could probably get him arrested, if you were clever,' he said, as they started home.

Jane laughed. 'Oh shut up, David. You read too many detective stories!'

'No, I mean it. If he's going to keep following you. If he, or one of his men, is waiting to pounce and carry you off and get you into the white slave trade, you should go to the police.'

'Don't be silly. What could I prove?'

'Well, nothing at the moment, but I bet the police know all about him. I bet they are longing to charge him. He's just been too clever for them – so far.'

Jane shuddered. She felt thoroughly unsettled. 'You don't know anything,' she said crossly. 'And I don't want to talk about it any more.'

They walked back in silence, but just as they slowed down to mount the steps to their front door, Jane crouched down to tie up her shoe-lace. She thought she'd seen him again and she wanted to make sure without arousing his suspicions.

'David,' she whispered. 'Don't look now. But that's Peter Daniels. He's standing on the corner with his back to us.'

David spilt some of the potatoes out of the bag on purpose and made a great show of bending down to pick them up. As he bent, he glanced furtively towards the corner.

At that moment, Peter Daniels turned round. Then, seeing that Jane and David were still on the doorstep, he turned abruptly away again. He had another man with him but, by the time Jane and David had replaced the potatoes in the bag, they had both disappeared.

'You're going to have to do *something*, Jane. He obviously knows where we live.'

'I know I have got to do something. But I can't think what.'

'Come on, let's go inside. I've got an idea.'

And, while Amy was preparing lunch, David explained.

'Look, we could go to the police and tell them the truth. Tell them that you traced Peter Daniels through the dressmaking business and that he's been following you, and that you think you know what he's up to.'

'And what then? I'd never . . .'

'Then,' interrupted David, 'you could offer to be a decoy.'

'A *decoy*! Whatever do you mean?'

David looked away from her and gazed out of the window. He said quietly, 'You could go out shopping, on your own, and see if he kidnapped you!'

'David! Don't be . . .'

'We'd have told the police,' he added hurriedly. 'Then they could follow you and arrest him when he kidnapped you!'

'Don't be ridiculous. Mum would never allow me to do that.'

'She doesn't have to know, does she?'

'She'd find out. She'd know something was up. And, anyway, the police would have to get her to agree, wouldn't they?'

David shrugged, then he glanced towards the kitchen. 'I don't think she's noticing anything much at the moment,' he said. 'She's worried about money.'

Jane frowned. 'She never said anything.'

'You've been away, Jane. She's been trying to find work, but it isn't easy. All she really knows about is running a hotel.'

'Why didn't she tell me?' repeated Jane.

'She hasn't said much to me, either. Just dropped a few hints. But she's anxious, I know that. The money won't last for ever and it's expensive living here in this flat, and paying school fees and everything.'

Amy came in at that moment and they changed the subject. Jane watched her carefully. David was right. She did seem anxious and distracted, though she tried not to show it.

When she went to bed that night, Jane thought again about David's idea. Would the police take them seriously if they told them about Peter Daniels? Perhaps, if they did, it would be a way of trapping him and convicting him. If they could do that, a lot of young women might be saved from a terrible life.

Was she brave enough to try it?

She yawned and fell into a deep sleep. She dreamt at first that she was back in Marlborough, with Anne and her father, but everywhere she went, Peter Daniels was there. She was riding in the pony and trap, urging the galloping Brandy to go faster and faster, but Peter Daniels was in a car beside them, easily keeping up.

And just as he was about to catch them, she woke up with a start, shaking with fear.

She sat up and hugged her knees. Perhaps they *should* go to the police. At least they would be doing something. She couldn't bear the thought of Peter Daniels creeping round after her all the time.

## Bedford, April, present day

*Katie and I went back to my house at lunch-time. I still couldn't eat and I knew that Gran thought I was sickening for something, but I managed to distract her, telling her that Mum had begun to speak. She and Grandad were so excited that they couldn't wait to go to the hospital and they didn't even ask what we were going to do in the afternoon.*

*As soon as they'd left the house, Katie and I fished out the envelope full of Keith's emails from under my mattress; I'd put it there in case Gran or Grandad came across it. As an afterthought, I found the stained threatening note Keith had sent Mum and she'd thrown away in the garbage bag. The police hadn't wanted to take it away. I stuffed that in the envelope, too. Then we set off to see Susan Bradfield.*

*Her office was in the middle of town and all the way there, on the bus, the envelope lay in my lap. I could hardly bear to touch it.*

*When we reached her office, I suddenly felt very scared. She was our last chance. If she couldn't help us, then I really didn't know what else we could do.*

*At last, a secretary came into reception and called my name. I clutched Katie's arm. 'Come in with me – please?'*

*'Sure,' said Katie, flashing me one of her big smiles.*

*She didn't need to come in with me. She didn't need to get involved in all this in the first place. But, without her, I don't think we'd have got anywhere.*

*'Thanks,' I whispered, trying to smile back.*

We went in. I didn't know Susan Bradfield well. She'd been to the house a couple of times, but that was all.

As soon as we walked in, she asked if Katie shouldn't wait outside, but I was firm. 'She knows everything. And . . . and she's helped me.'

Susan nodded. Then she said, 'Becky, I have to tell you that this isn't a professional visit. I'm seeing you as the daughter of a friend – that's all.'

I nodded. 'Matt and I didn't know who else to ask,' I said quietly.

She smiled then and asked us to sit down.

I tried to explain everything from the beginning, but it was a relief when she stopped me, mid-flow.

'I know a lot of this, Becky,' she said. 'Remember, your mum spoke to me when she was so worried about Matt.'

I nodded. Then I said, 'Did she tell you about the threatening note she got from Keith?'

'Yes, she told me about it, but she said she'd destroyed it and, if you can't produce it, it's simply your word against his.'

I fished in the envelope and brought it out. 'I dug it out from the rubbish,' I said, handing it over to her. 'Just in case we needed it. The police have seen it,' I added. 'Gran and Grandad got them round to the house yesterday.'

She smiled. 'Well done, Becky,' she said, taking it gingerly and reading it. 'Hang on to that. Handwriting experts can prove a lot these days. It could be valuable.'

I grinned and turned to Katie. 'Going through all that stinking rubbish was worth it after all,' I said.

Then I told Susan about the emails and handed over the worst of the bunch.

She looked at them carefully. I wondered how she could stand reading through all that filth. Katie and I sat still, watching her. I felt grubby, just knowing what she was reading. At last she looked up.

'Have you read these?'

I nodded. 'We just printed off some examples,' I said. 'There's lots more.'

She sat there, the emails lying in her lap, with her palms together and fingernails resting on her chin.

'Is it illegal?' I asked. 'Could he be charged for this?'

She didn't answer me directly. Instead she said, 'How did you get hold of all this?'

I hesitated. I wanted to tell her the truth but, if I did, we might be charged ourselves.

'We . . . I . . .' I began. But Katie interrupted me.

'We got the email address from Becky's mum's computer,' she said. 'Keith had sent her some emails a few weeks ago, before the accident.'

I looked at Katie, my eyes wide. I hoped no one was going to ask to see these non-existent emails!

Susan didn't appear to question this. 'What about the password?' she said.

'Oh, I remembered that he used Mum's name in it,' I said quickly. 'I experimented a bit and eventually I got it right.'

'Umm.'

I wasn't sure whether she believed me or not, but if she

really knew how we'd got the email address, she would probably refuse to help us. She probably thought it best not to question us too closely.

Slowly, she replaced the threatening note and most of the emails back in the envelope, but she kept a few back and continued to look at them.

'I'm pretty sure that these are child pornography sites,' she said quietly. 'And if they are, then I think the police would certainly want to interview Keith.'

I shuddered.

'But would they charge him?' asked Katie. 'Would they keep him away from Becky's family?'

'That is what worries me,' she said. 'My instinct is that with the emails and the threatening note, they should have enough to detain him, for his own safety and for yours. But we can't be sure.'

'Should we go to the police again, then?' I asked.

For answer, she nodded and picked up the phone. 'I know the local police,' she said. 'I'm coming with you. If they feel there's not enough to act – to search his house – then there's no harm done. By the way,' she added, 'do you know where he's living?'

I nodded.

'We heard him giving instructions to a cab driver,' said Katie quickly.

'And do the police know?' asked Susan.

'Er . . . no. I don't think so.'

Susan gave us a long stare and I thought she was going to

*question us further. But she didn't. She just punched a number into the phone.*

*'And if the police do agree to search his house?'*

*'If there's enough evidence here to convince the police, then we'll have to hope that they get to him before he gets suspicious.'*

*'Or gets to Mum,' I said quietly.*

### London, August 1947

The next day, Jane was very quiet. Although Amy was preoccupied, she noticed and asked if everything was all right.

'I'm a bit tired,' said Jane. 'I didn't sleep well last night.'

And it was true. She'd not gone to sleep at all after her nightmare.

As soon as she could, she spoke to David. 'I think you're right,' she said.

He knew instantly what she meant. 'Do you mean it? Are you prepared to go to the police?'

She nodded. 'I can't go on like this, terrified to leave the flat on my own.'

'They may not believe us,' said David, nervously.

And now it was Jane who was the determined one. 'I think we should try.'

David shrugged. 'Well, if Peter Daniels or his man

164

sees us going into a police station, at least he'll be frightened off and give up following you.'

'We don't *want* him to see us!' said Jane. 'We've got to give him the slip before we get to the police. That's the whole *point*! We've got to stop him doing this to other girls.'

'Oh. Well, yes. I suppose so.'

'David, what's the matter with you? It was your suggestion! I've been worrying all night about it. I'm prepared to risk being kidnapped, and you're getting cold feet!'

David frowned. 'No I'm not,' he said crossly. 'When shall we go?'

Jane glanced towards the kitchen. Amy was humming tunelessly as she washed up the breakfast dishes.

'Mum's going to see some man about a job this morning, so she'll be out. We could go as soon as she leaves the flat.'

'Okay,' said David, but he still looked worried. He paused, then continued. 'Are you *sure* you want to go through with this?'

'Yes I am,' snapped Jane. 'And I want to get on with it.'

A little later, Amy came into the room, dressed in her best suit and hat.

'You look very smart, Mum,' said Jane. 'What's the job you are going for?'

Amy looked down at her gloved hands. 'It's for a receptionist, dear. At a hotel not far from here.'

'A receptionist? But, Mum, you used to *run* the hotel in Melbourne.'

Amy looked irritated. 'That was then, Jane. This is now. And we need the money.'

Jane and David exchanged glances but said no more. They watched at the window until Amy had turned the corner and was out of sight, then they, too, left the flat.

'Do you know where we're going?' said David.

'Yes, I looked it up yesterday. It's only a couple of streets away.'

They walked in silence, Jane constantly looking from left to right.

'Can you see him?'

She shook her head. 'He can't be here every minute of the day, can he?'

But even so, they walked straight past the police station and went into a shop before doubling back. They ran up the steps and almost collided with a policeman coming down.

'Hey. Not so fast.'

'Sorry,' panted Jane, pushing the swing door which led to the lobby.

It was a forbidding place, with a large wooden counter which ran the length of one side of the room. Behind it, a uniformed policeman was writing something in a book. Behind him were shelves filled with files and between the shelves was a heavy door.

The counter was high and Jane could only just see over the top.

'Excuse me,' she said.

The policeman stopped writing and looked at them. 'Yes, Miss,' he said, quite kindly. 'What can I do for you?'

Now that she was here, Jane suddenly felt tongue-tied.

'My sister's being followed,' said David loudly.

The policeman smiled and continued writing.

Oh no, thought Jane. He's not going to believe us. She looked round at the other people sitting patiently on chairs set against the far wall. One man was twisting his trilby hat round and round in his hands, a woman was sniffing into a handkerchief and another man was mumbling quietly to himself.

'I need to speak privately to someone,' said Jane.

'Then you'll have to wait your turn, Miss,' said the policeman, without looking up.

Jane leant forward as far as she could, until her face was near the policeman's chest.

'The man following me,' she said clearly, 'is called Peter Daniels.'

She knew she'd got his attention then, because his pen stopped moving across the page. He looked up and met her eyes.

167

'Beg pardon, Miss. Who did you say?'

'Peter Daniels,' she repeated. 'He lives in Soho and . . .'

The policeman carefully put the top on his pen. 'Excuse me a moment,' he said, and went through the door behind the counter. He emerged a few moments later, looking serious. He opened up a flap in the counter and beckoned.

'Through here, please.'

Wordlessly, Jane and David followed him, behind the counter, through the door between the shelves, and then into another room. There was a more senior policeman there, also in uniform. He was sitting at a table, leafing through a file.

'Come in, sit down,' he said, as the first policeman left.

It was a long morning. First, Jane and David explained how Jane had discovered Peter Daniels, and why, and how she and Anne had visited him. Then, how she kept seeing him near the flat. Him and another man. Then the policeman questioned them carefully, asking all about their voyage from Australia, about Mum and about their father.

At last he seemed satisfied. He scraped back his chair and put his hands behind his head.

'Do you know what Peter Daniels does?' he asked Jane.

Jane looked embarrassed. 'Yes, I think so.'

David interrupted. 'He kidnaps girls and makes them become white slaves.'

David didn't really know what a white slave was, but it was something he'd heard at school.

The policeman smiled. 'Something like that,' he said. Then his face became serious. 'He's a very dangerous man,' he continued. 'And, although our colleagues in Soho are pretty certain about what he's doing, he's also very clever and they've never been able to pin anything on him. Once he's got girls working for him they are far too frightened to come to the police. He has a lot of pretty nasty thugs working for him, too. They are the ones who do his dirty work and he makes sure that they intimidate the girls.'

'Like the one he's got to follow me,' said Jane.

David butted in again. 'We wondered if Jane could be a decoy, Sir? Get herself kidnapped so you could follow her and find out where Peter Daniels takes the girls.'

The policeman tapped the file with his finger. Then he looked at Jane.

'Funnily enough,' he said, 'that idea had also occurred to me. Would you be brave enough to do that?'

Jane glanced at David. 'I think so. If . . . if I knew the police were watching me all the time.'

'Your mother would have to agree to it,' said the policeman.

'Oh, she'd never allow it!' said Jane.

'If she doesn't allow it, then we won't do it,' said the policeman firmly.

'Will you go and see her, then?' asked David.

The man shook his head. 'We don't want to arouse suspicions. I'll write her a note now for you to take her and I'll arrange to meet her somewhere to explain and try to get her permission.' Then he added, 'Did anyone see you coming here?'

David shook his head. 'I don't think so. We were really careful.'

The man spent a long time writing the note. When he handed it over, he said, 'We need to act fast. Daniels will give up if he can't get to you soon. He can't afford to have someone following you for ever.'

'What shall we do now?' asked David.

'I'll have someone show you the back way out of here and direct you back to your home. Then don't do anything until you hear from us. Don't go out on your own, Jane, until we tell you.'

As they left the building and scurried down the back streets the way they'd been directed, Jane held on to David's arm.

'I don't like this, David.'

David squeezed her hand. 'If it works, Jane, we'll have helped convict a criminal.'

'*If* it works!'

# Bedford, April, present day

*I'm writing this really late at night. I can't believe all that's happened today!*

*After we'd seen the police with Susan Bradfield, they were ready to spring into action. Katie and I had to go home and pretend we knew nothing.*

*The police had believed my story about remembering Keith's email address and his password and they'd seen all those horrible printouts and this time they'd taken the threatening note seriously. In fact, they'd taken it all very seriously.*

*It had helped, of course, having Susan with us. She was able to confirm what Mum had told her about Keith threatening us and threatening Matt.*

*I told them where Keith was living and they promised to search his house right away.*

*The waiting was terrible. I couldn't think of anything else except the police going to Keith's house. I snapped at Gran, even when she was telling me about their visit to Mum and how much better Mum seemed.*

*I even snapped at Katie. But at least she understood.*

*The afternoon dragged on. I kept looking at the clock but the minutes never seemed to go past.*

*It was well into the evening before we heard anything. I know the exact time; it was twenty minutes past seven.*

*My mobile rang and I snatched it up. It was Susan.*

*'Becky,' she said.*

'Yes! What's happened?'

'The police have charged him!'

I sank down to the floor, clutching the phone. I was shaking.

'Are you there, Becky? Did you hear me?'

'Yes,' I whispered. I knew I couldn't hold it together for much longer.

'He was there when they searched his house, Becky. And he went ballistic. He was off his head, trying to kill the police officer who showed him the search warrant.'

'Did they find enough to put him away?'

'Loads of stuff. Tapes, videos. Apparently it was well hidden, but the police pulled the place apart.'

I knew I couldn't hold back the tears much longer. 'Is he locked up – now, I mean?'

'Yes, he's in police custody and he's been seen by a psychiatrist.' She paused. 'He's a very sick man, Becky. Apart from all the vile porn stuff, he's too violent to be let out. He's going to a psychiatric hospital where he can get help.'

I started crying then, sobbing with relief and pent-up tension.

Gran found me, lying curled up on my bedroom floor, still shaking. She just held me. Held me for ages and waited until I could speak.

And when I could speak, I told her everything. She didn't interrupt once. She was brilliant.

And when I'd finished, she just said quietly, 'Have you told Matt?'

I hadn't. So we told him together.

# London, August 1947

Jane watched Amy's face as she read the note from the police. Watched it turn pale as she realized what she was being asked to agree to. She sank slowly into a chair and looked up at the twins.

'Why didn't you tell me about this man?'

Jane blushed. 'I didn't really know myself,' she said. 'Not for sure. Not until the police told us about him.'

'I can't let you do this, Jane,' said Amy. 'I can't put you in such danger.'

'I won't do it unless you let me,' said Jane. She was already regretting her hasty agreement to this hare-brained plan. If Mum refused to let her do it, then she needn't. And perhaps Peter Daniels and his horrible friends would leave her alone.

Or would they?

'At least go and talk to the policeman,' said David. 'They've been trying to get Peter Daniels for ages. It's a real chance for them to get the evidence against him that they need.'

'But using Jane as a *bait*! I can't allow that! It's too much of a risk.'

'People took greater risks in the war,' muttered David.

Amy shot him a horrified glance. 'But that was *war*, David. Nothing is the same in wartime.'

'And this is war, too – of a sort,' he replied. 'It's a war against something evil.'

'Don't be so melodramatic, dear,' said Amy, but they could see that she was affected.

'At least go and see the policeman, Mum,' said Jane, gently.

They both looked at her, waiting, holding their breath.

'All right,' she said at last. 'I'll go and see the man, but I'm very unhappy about this.'

'He'll be waiting there now,' said David.

Amy didn't answer. She put on her coat, hat and gloves, looked at the note again to check where she should go, and headed for the door.

'By the way,' she said, as she turned the handle, 'I've got the job at the hotel. The job as receptionist. I start after the school holidays.'


Amy wouldn't say what the policeman had told her, but she came back looking pale and shocked. The twins suspected he'd told their mother a lot more about Peter Daniels than he'd told them. All she would say was that he must be stopped.

'Does that mean that you'll let Jane do this?' asked David.

Amy looked at Jane. 'If she's willing to do it, then I won't stop her,' she said, choosing her words slowly. Then she went over to Jane and stroked her hair.

'Do you think I should do it, Mum?'

'Only if you want to, dear. And if you succeed, if they get Peter Daniels and his gang, you'll be saving a lot of girls and their families a lot of anguish.'

'And what if I fail?'

'If you fail then we shall know that we have at least tried our best to stop this dreadful man. And if anything goes wrong, the police will be right behind you. They've given me a route for you to take and they'll have plain-clothes police nearby watching you all the time.'

'What if no one tries to take me?'

'Then you are to keep trying for two more days. The same route, the same time.'

Jane swallowed. 'All right. Show me what I have to do.'

Jane didn't sleep at all that night and she was pale and jumpy when she left the flat at exactly ten o'clock in the morning.

Amy and David watched her go, Amy fighting back tears and David clenching and unclenching his fist.

Jane walked steadily along the route she had memorized. She visited the greengrocer and the butcher and bought food for the family. She had to queue at both shops and she glanced furtively about as she stood waiting her turn, but she couldn't see anything unusual. Peter Daniels' thug didn't seem to be around, but nor did any policemen. There was a young man reading a newspaper, standing beside a bicycle, with a cap pulled down. Could that be a policeman? She looked away quickly.

She glanced at her watch. She'd not been gone long, but she had several other calls to make. When the greengrocer handed over her package, she smiled and said she'd probably see him tomorrow. She did the same at the butcher's. Then she went on her way, calling into a couple of other shops, stopping to buy a paper from a newspaper boy, stopping to tie a shoe-lace.

She'd done all she was supposed to do, so she turned round and began to head for home. Her heart was thudding against her chest and she was sweating. She felt very frightened, especially now, when she was away from the crowded streets and back in the residential area. No one seemed to be about. If the police were watching her movements, they were doing it very discreetly.

At last she came in sight of the steps up to their front door and, forcing herself not to run the last few yards, she climbed up to the door and put the key in the lock. Once inside, she leant against the heavy frame and let out her breath.

Most of the time, everyone was on edge, waiting for something bad to happen. Amy was tense with worry,

David was unusually quiet and Jane just dreaded the next two days.

But when nothing happened on the second day, she began to relax. Perhaps Peter Daniels had given up and had some other girl in his sights now.

On the third morning, she felt better about it. She'd had a good night's sleep, it was a lovely day and all she had to do was follow the same routine one more time, then she could say she'd done her best.

As usual, she set off again at exactly the same time. She even turned round and looked up at the window of the flat, where she knew Amy would be standing, and waved.

She walked quickly through the quiet streets – where she thought there was most danger – and soon reached the shops. There were plenty of people around here and she felt much safer being part of a crowd. As usual, she tried to spot any plain-clothes police, but there was no one who stood out. Everyone seemed to be busy going about their business, scurrying here and there with only their own errands in mind.

Once again, she visited the greengrocer and got into conversation with the man serving her.

'You are getting to be one of my regulars, Miss,' he said, as he handed over a bag of apples and some broad beans.

Jane smiled. 'We've come to live round the corner,' she said, smiling. 'I expect I shall come here often.'

She felt quite relaxed. There was some good-natured jostling around her, but people were friendly and smiling in the late summer sunshine. All she had to do now was to walk on a little further and buy meat from the butcher, and then she could go home.

There was quite a crowd of people on the pavement near the greengrocer, and she had to push her way through, but she was glad of the press of bodies. They would protect her.

Then, suddenly, she lost her footing. As she dropped to her knees, spilling the contents of the brown paper bags, she wondered, momentarily, how it had happened. Was it an uneven paving slab? Had she tripped over someone's foot?

Irritated, she tried to get up again, but something was pressing on her leg. She twisted round to look and couldn't believe what she saw. A woman was standing on her! The woman had her leg pressed down firmly on the back of Jane's knee. Jane cried out with fury and tried to struggle free, but the woman pushed her down again, savagely, and then dropped down beside her. Before Jane realized what was happening, a handkerchief, smelling of something cloying and sickly, was being firmly held over her mouth and nose.

Her head began to swim. She tried to cry out. She tried to struggle free, but her voice wouldn't come out right and her arms and legs were immobile, leaden weights.

Through the waves of nausea and fear, Jane heard a woman's voice. It seemed to come from a long way away.

'Poor child. She does this sometimes. She's very given to fainting. It's the hot weather, you know. Just give us some space. It's nothing to worry about. My husband's got the car round the corner. We'll get her home and she'll be right as rain in no time.'

Jane tried to scream, but the sickening smell of whatever was on the handkerchief was making her lose consciousness and only a moan escaped her lips.

She realized in terror that she knew that voice! Her thoughts were confused and fragmented. Tap, tap, tap. Footsteps walking away down a hall. A voice on the phone. An aside to someone else: 'a bit young for you'.

Oh no! Please God, save me! Then everything went dark and still.

The crowd parted and Jane was dragged, a limp, helpless figure between a man and a woman, and bundled into a car which was conveniently parked only yards from the greengrocer.

The whole incident had taken less than a minute and, to the onlookers, seemed quite innocent. A young girl had fainted and was being cared for by her kind relations. No one thought, for one moment, that there was anything amiss.

\* \* \*

Jane started to come round several times on the journey, but every time she moved, someone clamped the vile-smelling stuff over her nose and mouth again and she passed out.

When she finally came to, she was sitting on a pile of blankets in a large darkened room and, as her eyes became adjusted to the gloom, she saw that there were several other young women in there with her. And, opposite her, stood Peter Daniels, one of his thugs, and the woman who had been in his house in Soho.

Jane couldn't stop trembling. Who would help her now? There was no sign of the police. No sound of doors being broken down, no shouting or demands to be let in.

They'd been too clever for the police! They'd given them the slip.

Jane opened her mouth and screamed, but the sound was stopped abruptly by a sharp slap across her face from the woman. Jane gasped with pain.

'No good screaming, my pretty one,' said Peter Daniels, with a smirk. 'No one will hear you. But if you're a good girl and do what you're told, we'll treat you nicely.' He addressed the other girls. 'Isn't that right, girls?'

There was a murmur of assent.

Jane looked around in amazement. All the girls had bowed heads. They were terrified. And then she saw the reason why. The thug had a whip in his hand and he was grinning. If anyone stepped out of line, she had no doubt at all that he would enjoy using it. Jane stared round her, horrified. This would be her future. No one would know she was here. She started to sob; great heaving uncontrolled sobs.

Peter Daniels put his face close to Jane's. 'Now, Jane. No hard work for you on your first day. Just a nice man who wants to meet you.'

Jane flinched and twisted away from him. 'Keep away from me!' she shouted through her sobs.

The girl nearest her touched her arm. 'Don't resist them. It's worse if you make a fuss,' she whispered.

'That's right,' said Peter Daniels, still smiling. 'You tell her to be a good sensible girl and nothing bad will happen to her.'

Then he and the woman suddenly lunged at her, took an arm each and started to drag her forward. Jane kicked out for all she was worth and caught Peter's ankle a sharp blow.

'Damn bitch!' he screamed, then he turned to his thug with the whip. 'Give her a taste of it!'

But as the thug raised his arm to lash out at her, Jane twisted away and the whip fell short.

Then, as he raised his hand again, there was suddenly a banging and crashing at the door.

'Police! We have the building surrounded.'

Things happened very fast, then. Jane cowered against the wall amid the noise and confusion. She covered her face with her hands, shaking with fright.

Then, after the screaming and shouting, came the sound of footsteps and the door banging shut again.

Someone touched Jane on the shoulder and she jumped with fright.

A policeman was crouching down beside her. 'Are you all right, love?'

She nodded, but she couldn't speak. The policeman gently helped her to her feet and led her out of the building.

## Marlborough, August 1947

The holidays were nearly over and Jane, Amy and David were all staying with Anne and her father.

Peter Daniels and all his associates had been rounded up by the police. Every one of the girls had agreed to testify against him, and he was in police custody awaiting trial.

Jane was the heroine of the hour. She felt a little bewildered by the praise which had been heaped on her – from the police in London, from Amy and David, but most of all from the Daniels brothers here in Marlborough. They had insisted on meeting her mother, and David, and giving them all presents and inviting them round.

One evening, the whole family had gathered. The

butcher and the saddler and all their families, together with Anne and her father and Amy and the twins.

Mr Daniels, the saddler, cleared his throat and everyone fell silent as he started to talk about their common ancestors, about Abbie and Jim – who became Henry Jones – about Amos and Seth, about Victoria and James, and all their descendants.

Amy was fascinated. How she wished that old Will could hear this.

And then, suddenly, Mr Daniels stopped and dug in his pocket. 'Come here, Amy,' he said. 'We've something for you.'

Amy stepped forward and took a small parcel from his outstretched hand.

'Not much survived after the house in East Smithfield was bombed in the Blitz,' he said. 'But we found this in the ruins and we'd like you to have it.'

Amy unwrapped the parcel. She took out a small gold snuffbox with a picture on the top. She turned it over and read the inscription on the back: '*Presented to the Honourable Percy Fanshaw by his fellow officers.*'

'Oh,' she cried, 'I know all about this. Old Will told me. He told me when he gave me the watch. He said that Jim had been wrongly accused of stealing the watch and sent to Tasmania for six years for a crime he didn't commit. And then he went back to London and it was there that he *did* steal things – including this snuffbox!'

'Yes, we heard that, too, and we thought they should stay together,' he said. 'The watch and the snuffbox.'

Mr Daniels smiled and looked at his brother, who nodded approval.

## Marlborough, December 1950

It was a particularly happy Christmas for Anne and Jane. In the autumn, Amy had given up the hotel receptionist job, which she had always hated, and married Anne's father. She and Jane had come to live in the cottage near Marlborough and Amy was helping to get the musical instrument business on its feet again. The little cottage was bursting at the seams and soon they would have to find somewhere bigger.

David had gone back to Australia to finish his education; he had enjoyed his time in England, but he pined for the beaches and the heat and the wide open spaces.

The cold wind howling outside made them feel snug and safe and highlighted their warmth and companionship. After they had eaten the Christmas turkey, Anne's father made them all drink a toast.

'To absent friends,' he said.

Everyone stood up. 'To absent friends,' they chorused, raising their glasses.

And, briefly, they were each silent with their own

thoughts. Jane thought of David, spending his Christmas with relatives in Australia, and of her father, buried in a foreign jungle. And she thought of old Will, too, lying at peace in the well-tended cemetery in South Yarra.

Anne and her father thought of Anne's mother, loved and never forgotten.

And Amy. Amy thought of all these; and of Ernest Liddle, too.

'To them all,' she said quietly.

'To them all,' they repeated.

## Bedford, August, present day

*Mum came home today. She's still weak and sometimes she's confused, but she looks wonderful and it's fantastic to have her back.*

*Matt came up from London and we had some friends in, and the house was full of presents and flowers.*

*Gran and Grandad are still here and they're going to stay on for a bit. They've been incredible but they want to get back to their own home now.*

*Mum still can't remember anything about the accident, so I guess we'll never know what really happened that night. But she knows that Keith is in the psychiatric wing of a high-security hospital and likely to remain there. She knows she's safe now.*

*Amazingly, she doesn't hold a grudge against him. Just says he was obviously very sick.*

*I wonder if I'll ever be able to be as forgiving?*

*Mum was tired, so she went to bed early, but Matt and I stayed up, talking to Gran and Grandad. When Gran was out in the kitchen, I suddenly remembered something I'd wanted to ask both of them.*

*'Grandad?' I said. 'Ages ago, we found this gold watch and a little snuffbox in the attic. Mum said they'd come from Gran's family. Can you tell me about them?'*

*Grandad smiled and yelled towards the kitchen.*

*'Jane!' he shouted. 'Stop fiddling in the kitchen and come in here and sit down. Becky wants to know about the watch and the snuffbox.'*

*Gran came in, wiping her hands on a tea-towel. 'Oh goodness,' she said. 'That really is ancient history. It's a very long story. Are you sure you want to hear it now?'*

*'Yes,' I said firmly. 'Otherwise I'll forget to ask again.'*

*So Gran settled herself in an armchair and began.*

*It was very late when she'd finished, but it was then that I made a decision.*

*I know what I'm going to do in my gap year now. I'm going to save up and go to Australia to visit Gran's twin brother and all the relations in Melbourne.*

*Maybe I'll be able to persuade Katie to come with me.*